Praise for

I0536999

Praise for

The Chameleon

". . . an intricate, fast-paced novel of many surprises, villains at every turn and difficult choices. Ms. Burton has done an excellent job world-building. I was thoroughly engrossed in the book to the very last page and was rewarded with a fairy-tale ending. A highly-recommended read.

~ best-selling author Marilyn Baron

The Pilot

"I love Diane Burton's spunky heroine, and the humor of the story. An exciting, fast paced adventure with a satisfying romance. If you love outer space and romance, this is the book for you."

~ Award-Winning author Alicia Dean

Switched, Too

"A thrilling tale . . . that will fill the imagination, leaving the reader wanting more with each page turned!"

~ Melody Prat, *InD'tale Magazine*

Switched

"Who knew science fiction could be so sassy, sexy, and fun?" ~ Nancy Gideon, bestselling author of the By Midnight Series

Also by Diane Burton

Switched

Switched, Too

Switched Resolution

The Pilot (An Outer Rim Novel)

The Chameleon(An Outer Rim Novel)

The Protector (An Outer Rim Novel)

Numbers Never Lie, a Romantic Suspense

*The Case of the Meddling Mama: An Alex
O'Hara Novel*

*The Case of the Fabulous Fiancé: An Alex
O'Hara Novel*

*The Case of the Bygone Brother: An Alex
O'Hara Novel*

How I Met My Husband (contributor)

*Portals: Volume 2: Gateway to the Worlds
of Science Fiction Romance* (contributor)

MISSION TO NEW EARTH

a novella

Diane Burton

This is a work of fiction. Names, characters, places and incidents are the product of the author's imagination or are used fictitiously. Any resemblance to actual persons, living or dead, events, or locales is entirely coincidental.

Copyright © 2018 by Diane Burton

Excerpt from *The Protector* copyright © 2015 by Diane Burton

Cover design by The Novel Difference

All rights reserved. No part of this publication may be reproduced, distributed, or transmitted in any form without the prior written permission of the author.

ISBN- 978-0-9990452-1-3

Dedication

To my children for their continued love
and support

To my grandchildren whose giggles
brighten my day

And especially to Bob, my best friend
and hero

Acknowledgements and Thanks

Thank you to the members of the Mid-Michigan chapter of Romance Writers of America® for their continued support and advice. To Alicia Dean for her editing of this work and to my critique partner, Alison Henderson. Their help made this story better. To Florence at The Novel Difference for the amazing cover art. Thank you, ladies.

Most importantly, I want to thank my family for all their support. Liz & Matt, Doug & Katy, I'm very proud of you. Thank you for encouraging me.

To my husband, Bob. How glad I am that our friends fixed us up on that blind date!

T minus 4 days and counting

I thought this week would never arrive. Yet, it came too soon. Are we ready? If we had another week, month, year, would we be ready?
Too late now.

"Simulation complete," the technician sitting next to me announced.

I was in the control booth where I'd watched my team perform the landing on our new planet. A tad bumpy landing but one we could all easily survive. Normally, I was with my team instead of watching them. Director's orders, which never set well with me. I was a do-er not a watcher.

As I waited for confirmation from the director, seconds ticked by slower than a melting glacier. The question kept running through my mind. *Are we prepared?* They shortened our training. Four years instead of eight. *My God, what did they leave out?*

"Commander Grenard." Director Ashcroft rose stiffly. The sim had lasted more than two hours. His knee joints protested his lengthy sedentary position by popping. "Your team passed the landing simulation."

I slowly released a breath, when I really wanted to jump up, hug everyone in the booth, and do a happy dance. Instead, I nodded. "Thank you, sir. I'll share your words with the team."

As I got up, the technician winked. "Nice job, Sara."

I smiled. Of all the techs, Roland was the most supportive. He'd been with our team all four years, starting in New Mexico. Back then, we thought we had eight years to prepare. Four years at White Sands before moving to Ares Station on Mars. But a catastrophe prompted the move to Ares two years sooner. We spent a year there instead of two before moving to Titan. Despite Director Ashcroft's reassurance, I worried. I feared for my team.

We were about to leave on an adventure of a lifetime. All right, not just us. Two other teams were ready, too. Just thinking about how fortunate we were to explore possible new homes for Earth's inhabitants, I was still awestruck. Giddiness raced through me and with it the ever-present trepidation. What could go wrong? Were we prepared for all eventualities? What if—

I had to stop speculating on the dangers of our mission. My fear could easily infect my team and spread worse than the bout of influenza that devastated three teams before we left Ares. I was certain the other commanders didn't have my fears. Yuri and Kaito always seemed calm and matter-of-fact about our missions. I bet they didn't have a swarm of bees roiling around in their stomachs.

Speeding down the corridor, I passed holiday decorations. The festive trimmings brightened the gray walls. When we arrived at Titan Station, I was too excited to notice the all-gray atmosphere. After eleven months here, I wanted to strangle the interior decorator. I hoped the modules deposited on Serenity had a better paint job.

Serenity. Our hope for the future of our new planet. After screwing up Earth, humankind had the chance to do it right this time. Unlike Mars, with its constant influx of inhabitants, Serenity would start slow, only the six of us. A year from now, the ship leaving supplies on the closest planet would return, and the next six would leave Titan. Each time a supply ship returned, another team could leave.

Unless another crisis on Earth occurred.

If they'd stuck to the original timeline, we would lead a group of three hundred pioneers, specialists of all kinds. But the mega-ships weren't ready. Though manufacturers worked around the clock, they couldn't produce the ships necessary to transport that number of people.

Those ships would have been ready had our mission stayed on schedule.

Consequently, our long-distance vehicles could only carry a team of six at a time. After we reached Serenity, our ship would return for our next team . . . six years after beginning its first voyage. If our planet proved habitable.

Everything moved up after the latest disaster on Earth. As if overpopulation and depletion of resources weren't enough, an earthquake in the mid-Atlantic created a tsunami greater than any in history. The tsunami wiped out cities along the Eastern seaboard up to eighty miles inland. So many lives lost, despite the early warning system. Riots and the worst of human behavior destroyed more.

Could the people on Earth survive any more catastrophes?

As I rounded a corner, I nearly collided with Kaito. Uttering a quick apology, I skirted around him.

"Wait up, Sara-san."

Although my team waited for me, I stopped. Kaito Tanaka, tall and handsome with a ready laugh and charming demeanor, had been my competitor, now an ally. He wore the bright red jumpsuit with such a confident air everyone could see why he was a team leader.

"I hear your sim went well."

"Thanks, Kaito-san. When does yours start?"

He groaned. "As soon as they reset the program. My team dreads the landing sim more than all the others."

"We had a bumpy landing. You might consider slowing the descent as much as possible. We were too anxious."

With a mock-formal bow, he said, "Arigato, Sara-san."

"You're welcome, Kaito-san. Good luck." I returned his bow then took off toward the habitat wing.

I was surprised my team wasn't there yet. When I turned back toward the Admin corridor, Marsh strode toward me with determination—so different from that easy-going swagger that caught my eye the first time I saw him four years ago at the White Sands Training Center. I never believed in love at first sight, but oh, mama. With dark-haired, dark-eyed Marsh, I fell hard. I must've done a great job hiding my feelings back then. He said he never knew—until a year later when I pinned him on the exercise mat and kissed him. Yep, I took the initiative and planted a toe-curling smooch on his delectable lips. Not to be outdone, he kissed back. Holy smoke. If I'd known what a great kisser he was, I'd have done it sooner. He said he'd been biding his time, waiting for me to catch up. According to him, one look into my "gorgeous blue eyes" and he was a goner, too.

"We need to talk," he said as he blasted past me toward our quarters.

What? I looked around. Where was the rest of my team? Marsh took an impatient whack at the mistletoe ball hung from a garland. Oh, boy. What had gotten into him?

Bill and Tom trailed behind Marsh with Gloria and Ana bringing up the rear. Like me, they wore forest green jumpsuits, and they did not look pleased. Glum was a better word.

The last simulation wasn't *that* bad. A couple of glitches with last minute corrections. Maybe a reminder to one person or another. I thought we did well. Glitches happened. No need for concern. Or was there? What didn't I know?

Bill hung back and waited for me to catch up. "He's right. We need to talk without Big Brother listening."

The last he delivered in a whisper with a wink and a nudge. Since we were close in height, he didn't have to bend down, just leaned his ginger head next to my dark one. Loved that term ginger for hair color. Doctor Who always wanted ginger hair. Bill often reminded me of that classic sci-fi show from the late 20th century.

I tried not to smile at his reference to George Orwell's *1984*, required reading in my elementary school. Considering all the cameras located throughout the station, Big Brother was an appropriate appellation.

"I assume Marsh has a place in mind?" I matched my stride to Bill's, the most easy-going of our team. Bill was a guy's guy. Best friend to everyone.

"Yeah, he does."

Good thing. We couldn't just take a walk outside, unless we could breathe methane. Titan was a trifle inhospitable. In preparation for our mission, the United Earth Space Agency established Saturn's largest moon as our launch platform. Connected habitats, added before we arrived, evolved into crew quarters, conference and training rooms, and general meeting areas. We weren't absolutely sure, but we thought our quarters were monitored—something I'd queried but received no definitive response. None of us were happy about that. But then in four days, we'd be on camera all the time. That was the second worst thing I feared about our voyage.

As we followed, Marsh strode across the corridor to the left. The only private place down there was a lavatory. Not my favorite destination for a team meeting. But beggars couldn't be choosers, as my mom used to say.

"We screwed up again," Marsh announced as soon as the five of us joined him. His voice echoed off the hard surfaces. "In RT, it could kill us."

"You and your damn RT," Tom spat out. "Why can't you just say *real time* like a normal person?"

Marsh shot him a look, one I'd hate to have directed at me.

Military background evident, he stood in the middle of the area near the showers, his feet wide apart, hands clasped behind his back. The others were more casual. Bill held up a white-tiled wall across from the showers. Ana and Gloria sat on a fake wood bench. Meanwhile, I crossed my arms and leaned against a sink. I tried to look casual even though my nerves were strung tight. We had to be ready for the launch. Earth was depending on us.

All of my team, except Tom and Marsh, wore hang-dog expressions. At forty, six years older than me, Tom was the oldest on the team and a damn fine pilot. His red face and mutinous expression as he confronted Marsh belied his usually even-keeled manner.

"You're exaggerating, Rayburn." That was more than angry. Tom was defiant. "You always exaggerate. Worst case scenario? Is that all you think about?"

I'd never seen Tom so worked up. Gloria walked over to him and rubbed his shoulder. Usually in stressful times, her gentle caress calmed him down. Not now.

When he shrugged off her hand, I caught the hurt in her eyes.

"C'mon, Bill. Back me up on this."

Bill held out his hands in a don't-get-me-involved gesture. He was our engineer, both formal and practical. He could fix anything from wonky engines to food replicators.

Tom turned to me. "Sara?"

I knew that was coming. I tried to let my team work things out by themselves. Soon we'd be living in close confines, not just on the ship but on our Goldilocks planet. If we couldn't live in harmony during training, we would be in deep trouble once we reached our final destination. We'd be in even worse trouble if we couldn't work out our differences here. Marsh was right to pick the only place that wasn't monitored. We absolutely didn't want the directors to think we weren't a well-functioning team.

They could pull us and put in the Shadow Team. Our replacements.

"Okay, guys, what did I miss?" With a forced grin, I raised my right hand. "I swear I wasn't dreaming about a day at the beach during the sim."

Bill and Gloria laughed out loud. They knew how much I missed my California sun and surf. Intense, serious-minded Ana cracked a smile. Tom didn't. Marsh just stared unrelentingly.

He stood ramrod straight, another leftover from his military training. "Slow reflexes, poor timing, and lackadaisical attitudes. And that's just for starters. If that sim had been RT, we would all have been killed. Thanks to you, Warfield."

"Why you—" Tom would have clocked him if Gloria hadn't gripped his arm.

"Whoa." Bill pushed away from his wall. "Hey, Marsh, why don't you tell us how you really feel?"

Marsh, who'd taken a defensive stance in preparation for Tom's blow, didn't back down. He didn't even move.

"Okey-dokey." I stepped between them, hoping one of them didn't let loose and clock me. "Let's bring this down a notch. C'mon, guys. It's the holidays. Let's have some good cheer. We're a team. Remember? An *effective* team."

Bill snorted. A movie aficionado like me, he got the reference to a long-ago film.

Marsh shrugged and walked over to the opposite wall where he leaned his shoulder against it. Maybe the cold tile would cool him off. From his tightly crossed arms, I doubted that.

If this were a cartoon, steam would be coming out of Tom's ears. By the way Gloria clutched his arm, her worry had escalated along with the tension. Bill eyed the other two men with a wariness that was unusual for him. Ana hadn't moved from her seat on the bench. As usual, she took everything in without comment and processed it all before drawing conclusions or making judgments. Sometimes I wished she would let loose. Scream and holler like the rest of us. A futile wish, I knew.

Or maybe it was better to have at least one cool head among us. God knew, I had to rein in my temper enough times. As team leader, I was supposed to set an example. Yeah, right. I wanted to deck both men.

Here's the thing. If they screwed up, if the directors sensed dissention, our team could be replaced even at this late date. The Shadow Team, who were supposed to go next year, would be only too happy to take our place. If they learned about our mini-meltdown, they would report it. Especially if it meant they could go instead of us.

"The landing was a tad bumpy," I said. "But—"

"A tad?" Straightening away from the wall, fists clenched, Marsh glared at me. "More than just a *tad*. If our pilot didn't have his head up his butt—"

Tom twisted away from Gloria, a murderous look in his eyes.

Again, I stepped between the men. Again, I hoped I wouldn't get a fist in the face. Still, I had to keep the two men apart. "Look, guys. Ashcroft was pleased with our performance. But . . . I'll get read-outs on our reaction times and compare them to previous exercises. Will that satisfy you two?" I looked from Marsh to Tom.

Neither man gave an inch. Well, shoot. The tension in the lavatory was palpable. We couldn't leave until our attitudes returned to normal. If The Weasel saw us, he was sure to tattle.

"Listen up, folks. From my vantage point, the landing looked to be a success. You didn't crash. That's a good point, right?" I looked around at the five before blowing out a breath. "I think we're so confident in our duties that we're getting a little complacent. All this extra training is doing more harm than good. We need a break. Downtime until tomorrow morning."

"We need more training," Marsh insisted. "With the timetable ramped up, we can't be lax."

"We know the basics." I hated arguing with Marsh. As well as our second-in-command, he was my partner. My lover.

My loyalty had to be toward the team.

Tom looked at me. "The schedule says—"

I fixed him with my best leader's stare—the one Marsh compared to shards of ice. "I don't give a rip what the schedule says. We need downtime. I'll take care of things with the *Powers That Be*. You guys go somewhere and chill."

"All right." Bill pumped the air with his fist. "You give the *PTB* what for, Sara. C'mon, Ana baby. I know what we can do during our downtime." He pulled Ana to her feet.

Though blushing, she didn't protest.

Gloria put her arms around Tom's neck. Being six inches shorter, she had to stand on her tiptoes to whisper in his ear. A slow smile twitched his lips. When he nuzzled her neck, a pink blush flooded her fair complexion. She clasped his hand and led him out of the restroom.

Then only Marsh and I were left.

I strolled up to the man I loved and put my arms around his waist. When I rested my head on his chest, I heard the thud of his heart. Normally, a reassuring sound that always made me go weak in the knees, it beat more rapidly than usual. He was still agitated.

"Hey, guy. Everything will be all right. We're ready. More than ready."

"I know. It's just—"

Leaning back in his arms, I reached up and patted his cheek. "Settle down, big boy. I think Bill and Ana have the right idea. From Gloria's blush, she and Tom do, too." I gave him a long kiss. At first, he didn't respond—still worked up over the latest simulation. Then he gave in, as I knew he would. Not to be smug, but Marsh did like my kisses.

His kiss turned hard, demanding, as he strained to maintain control. I wanted him that much, too. But not on the tile floor in the lav. The shower had possibilities. When he eyed the enclosure, I knew he was thinking the same thing. Too bad I had other obligations. That was me, duty first. I could be such a stick-in-the-mud.

"I have to talk to Director Ashcroft about the change in schedule." I couldn't look at Marsh. If I did, I'd lie down on the narrow bench and beg him to have his wicked way with me. "Meet me in our room in ten minutes."

"Make it five, and I'll buy dinner." He gave me a crooked smile.

I knew exactly what he planned for dessert. "Ha ha. All meals are included at this fabulous vacation resort."

Marsh snorted.

"I can dream, can't I?" I grinned up at him. "White sandy beach, gentle tropical breezes. Sun." How I missed the warmth of the sun on my face. Seeing it through heavy plexi-glass windows wasn't the same. Neither was breathing filtered air instead of fresh.

"Want me to go with you to see Ashcroft?"

As second-in-command, he normally attended meetings with me. Not a good idea this time. Not with the tension still rippling through his body.

I stroked his tight jaw. "I can handle it."

Reluctantly, he released me. "Got get 'em, Tiger."

With a laugh, I headed back to the admin wing. I passed Roland who gave me a thumbs up. "How many hours, Sara?" the technician called over his shoulder. Same question he asked every time I saw him.

"Too many," I responded as I usually did. Or not enough, as I usually thought.

Ashcroft was in his office, head down, intently scrutinizing a printout. I rapped on his half-opened door. He looked up, took off his glasses, and pinched his nose. "Come in. Come in." He sounded impatient. Probably not the best time to tell him my decision to give my team time off.

"Problems, sir?"

He gestured for me to sit. With all the advances in science, furniture makers should have figured out how to make comfortable visitor chairs. Or maybe the *Powers That Be* decided that uncomfortable chairs would force the visitor to quickly get to the point.

"Paperwork," he responded in disgust. "If I had a nickel for every report, chart, and diagram I have to send to Ares as well as White Sands, I'd be wealthy."

I chuckled. I heard that complaint every time I saw him. "That's why you're making the big bucks, Jim."

He snorted, scrawled a note on the sheet before him, then folded his hands on his slight paunch and leaned back. His chair squeaked in protest. "What do you need, Sara?"

After scooting to the edge of the seat, I said, "I gave my team time off until tomorrow morning."

"But the next simulation—"

"Look, Director. It is not our fault your superiors moved up the launch." When he started to protest, I held up my hand. "Not yours, either. Jim, we're exhausted. You cannot work the teams eighteen hours a day."

"Hardly eighteen, Sara."

I brushed that aside. "You said we're ready. I agree. We need a break. A well-deserved break." I stared at him, daring him to disagree.

After a pause, he sat forward and fiddled with his glasses. I was always surprised to see anyone wearing glasses. He should have had his vision rectified as an infant.

"All right. I trust your judgement, Sara."

He damn well better. Otherwise, he shouldn't have appointed me—the geology specialist—team leader. I waited, not very patiently as I clenched my hands so hard my short nails poked into my palms.

He pursed his lips. "Your team is scheduled for one more sim. The timeline—"

"The hell with the timeline." I stood. "It's in my team's best interest that we delay that last sim until tomorrow. Sir," I tacked on since I was pushing insubordination.

"Commander—"

"We'll ace the sim—as we aced every sim—tomorrow at ten. See you at dinner." I left before he could come up with any more objections.

As I made my way down the corridor to our quarters, I stopped at the narrow walkway between the Admin section and Crew Quarters. As I usually did, I looked out the viewport. Through the lighter-than-normal smog, I searched for landmarks.

"Hi, ho, Commander." Our medical android sauntered up to me. "Whatcha looking at?"

When Medical Technician 447 renamed herself MT, she told us she liked the play on her initials, though her mechanical brain was far from empty. Her manufacturer had designed her to look human with short, curly black hair, and a small, slender body. What they hadn't counted on was her ability to find humor in most situations. She added a sparkle to our lives. I was glad she would travel to Serenity with us. Too bad she wouldn't stay.

"Come on, Commander. Scooch over so I can see." She hip-bumped me.

I sidestepped, even though we both had enough room. "I think I see the hills of Xanadu."

"Near the equator?" She scrunched up next to me to peer through the porthole. "Nope. We're too far away."

"Well, darn."

"Hang on." MT cupped her hands around her eyes and leaned closer to the window. "If you look close, you can see Sotra Patera."

"Really." I'd never seen the mountain before. Cupping my hands like she did, I tried and failed. "You have better eyes than me, MT."

"No shit, Sherlock." She clapped her hands over her mouth. "Sorry."

"You have to stop repeating Bill's smart aleck remarks." I grinned to let her know I wasn't mad at her. "I'll keep looking for landmarks. Maybe the smog will clear."

"Don't bet on it." MT sauntered away with what my dad called 'a hitch in her giddiup.'

I tried again to see the cryovolcano through the smoggy atmosphere. This land was as foreign as that around Ares Station. From the pictures sent back by the probe of the Earth-like planet we named Serenity, our new home would look as natural as Earth itself. I wanted so badly to believe the reports that the surface would have breathable air, that we would be able to walk outside without our enviro suits, that we could live there as we lived on Earth. After two years in an enclosed environment, I was going a little stir-crazy. More than a little. Being an outdoor girl, cabin fever had hit me a lot sooner than the others. I silently groaned. I *used* to be an outdoor girl.

So how did a California beach girl like me end up on Saturn's moon, preparing to make history? It was a long story, best reserved for a starlit night in front of a campfire overlooking the dark waters of the sea, and accompanied by a cool glass of wine. With Marsh by my side, of course. Even he didn't know my whole story. Just like I didn't know his or the rest of my team's. We all had our reasons for joining the mission.

The short version: I volunteered. Slightly longer version: my parents died in a car accident; teaching bratty kids sucked, especially when a kid eight inches taller and a hundred pounds heavier attacked me, and the principal didn't support me. Believe me, I was ready for a change.

And what a change.

I never imagined I'd be selected. Not when over fifty thousand applied within ten hours. Or so I heard. Out of five hundred thousand applicants, the eighteen of us became the chosen teams. Oh, not as easy as that. The tests they put us through—physical, psychological, intellectual—still boggled my mind.

And I used to think teaching high school kids with more money than smarts was a challenge. Nothing prepared me for the adventure of a lifetime.

Being a pioneer.

* * *

Marsh was waiting for me in our bed, his electronic reader propped against his broad chest. God, I loved looking at him. Especially when he was naked. I'd had my share of romantic relationships. But never like what Marsh and I had.

Besides being a fine-looking man and intelligent, he was strong-willed without a major ego. When I was appointed team leader, his congratulations were sincere as he accepted second place. Since then, he'd been my biggest supporter. And my lover.

Lover. I never thought of a man that way before. In my other relationships, so few I could count them on one hand, the guys were boyfriends or friends with benefits. Not Marsh. He was special. I would spend the rest of my life with him.

The rest of my life. That made me pause.

Who knew how long the rest of our lives would be? We could live into old age in a place far, far away. Or we could all die on launch. In cryo. On landing. Or—

"How did Ashcroft like your decision?" Marsh cut off my morbid thoughts.

Better not to think about all that could go wrong on our mission. We were told the risks. In the excitement of being chosen, who really listened to the warnings? As launch time came closer, those warnings crept into my mind with greater frequency.

Why was I dredging up dark thoughts when my love lay waiting for me?

With the usual ripping sound, I pulled apart the closure of my jumpsuit. "How do you think?"

He whistled that old tune "The Stripper" just like he always did.

I grinned as I shimmied out of the one-piece suit then toed off my soft-soled shoes before I tripped. Down to my underwear, I picked up the discarded dark green jumpsuit and twirled it. With a seductive smile, I tossed it to Marsh.

He flipped it on the floor. "Oh yeah, baby. Take it off. Take it all off."

I rolled my hips in hula moves I learned in college on the Big Island. A slow shimmy later, I clasped the bottom of my support camisole and slowly raised it over my head.

"Is this what you had in mind?" Half-naked, I stood hip-shot before I twirled the cami and tossed it to him.

"You're killing me, babe. Hurry up."

I hooked my thumbs in my bikini panties and slowly lowered them until they covered only the absolute necessity. When he groaned, I turned my back to him before dropping them. Looking over my shoulder, I winked. "Do you want the panties, too?"

"No." He growled. "Just you."

T minus three days and counting

At breakfast, we all appeared refreshed. I hoped I didn't look as satisfied as the other five. A couple of times, we looked at each other and smirked.

Ashcroft's monitor minions probably told him exactly how we'd spent our downtime.

The sims went better than ever. Afterward, Director Ashcroft met us in the small conference room next to his office. In an attempt to identify with space pilots, Ashcroft called it his ready room. While a first-class supervisor, he walked a tight rope between placating the teams and kowtowing to his own bosses back at Mission Control.

We sat around the oval table waiting for the verdict, our posture reflecting our personalities. Bill slouched while Ana tensed. Tom was usually relaxed but not today. He looked wary. Next to him, Gloria appeared wide-eyed and eager, as always. She was our doctor and my best friend. Marsh sat up straight, like he had a stick up his butt. Me? I was somewhere between Bill and Marsh. Then throw in some of Ana's tension and Gloria's eagerness and you have a mass of contradictions and nerves. With confidence earned dealing with teens, I folded my hands on top of the faux wood table and waited.

Jim cleared his throat. "You did well. Good response time."

"Good?" I raised my eyebrow. Technician Roland had shared that our response time surpassed the other two teams.

"Better than before," Ashcroft conceded.

I accepted that and forced myself not to say "I told you so" about our unscheduled downtime.

If we were better than before—better than the other two teams, why no smile?

Jim clasped and unclasped his hands. "Commander, it is my duty to ask. Is your team ready?"

With pride nearly bursting out of me, I glanced around the table at my team before answering. "Absolutely, sir."

For the first time since operations moved to Titan Station, he appeared nervous. "I, uh, heard there was a problem yesterday." He looked pointedly at Tom.

Oh, shit.

Before Tom opened his mouth, I said, "No problem, sir."

Ashcroft looked from Tom to me a couple of times, partly suspicious, mostly relieved. "Good. Good. This mission is of the highest priority." As if we weren't aware of that. "With Earth's over population and dwindling resources, we need alternatives. The latest crisis makes it imperative—"

As one, we all straightened. "What crisis?"

From the expression on Jim's face, I guessed he wasn't supposed to tell us. When he wiped sweat off his forehead, despite the moderate temperature, I was certain The Powers wanted to keep that quiet.

Jim blew out a breath. "Scientists have detected a potential supervolcano in the Indian Ocean."

"Oh, shit." Bill slumped. "Volcanic winter."

"What?" Ana exclaimed. "I don't understand."

Bill clasped her hand. "When massive amounts of ash and debris are spewed into the atmosphere, it will cloud the sun, reduce global temperatures. Crops won't grow. Radiation—"

"Hold on," Jim said. "They don't know how long it will take to erupt above the surface. Or even if it will."

"But what are they doing to prepare the people?" I asked. "Do we have enough time to find a new home? For everyone?"

Jim didn't speak. His non-answer was an answer itself. That scared me more than if he'd come right out and said "no."

How much time did humans have left on Earth?

Jim continued, "Preparations are being made for people to move underground until a massive exodus can occur."

"Then the scientists must be sure that the supervolcano will explode." Bill spoke so matter-of-factly I was even more frightened. Not for myself. I wouldn't be there. I feared for the billions left on Earth.

"Did you say underground?" Gloria asked. "Like in caves?"

Jim nodded. "Natural and manmade."

It was bad enough to live above ground in habitats with artificial air. I couldn't survive stuck in a cave emotionally. I knew I couldn't. Well, maybe. If my life depended on it . . .

"What about bio-domes?" Marsh asked.

Again, Jim nodded. "They're preparing for the worst." He cleared his throat. "So you see why your mission must succeed. Yours and the other two teams."

It was worse than I thought. Worse than any of us thought.

"What about our families?" Bill asked.

He had a sister in Montana with three kids. Gloria had several nieces and nephews. Marsh's entire family lived in Nebraska—his parents, a sister, several brothers, and a slew of little kids. As far as I knew, Tom and Ana were like me. We had no one.

"You were promised when you signed on for this mission that your families would be given priority over the average citizen. We all were given that assurance." Jim had family, too, back on Earth. "Now, Planets 2247, 6719, and 4434 are our best possibilities for homes. I can tell you that, before you land on Planet 4434, the big ships should be ready. Are you?"

He stared at each of us in turn, lingering longer on Tom.

"I can say with certainty—" Marsh spoke with quiet assurance. "—this team is ready."

"I agree," I said. "And, by the way, Planet 4434's name is Serenity."

Each team was given the honor of naming our destination planet. We wanted the name to reflect our hopes for the future of our new homeland. The Asian team named Planet 2247 Hope, and the Euro-African team named 6719 Peace.

"Yes, yes. Of course. Serenity." Ashcroft appeared befuddled. I couldn't imagine why. He'd known the correct designations for months.

I had to find out why. "Is there a problem? I mean, besides what's going on back home?"

He stood. "Good job on the simulations, folks. Now I wish to speak to Sara."

The others looked at me. From their expressions, they seemed as confused as I was about this turn of events. In the past, he'd always talked to us as a team, rarely to me separately. I gave them a brief nod, and all but Marsh filed out. He stood behind me, his hands on the back of my chair. His stance said plainer than words he had my back.

"Captain Rayburn, you may leave." Ashcroft gave him a pointed look.

Marsh squeezed my shoulder then left. I swiveled my chair sideways, crossed my legs, and clasped my hands loosely in my lap—a casual position, so Ashcroft couldn't see how worried I was. "All right, Jim, what else is going on?"

He plopped into the chair at the head of the table. For a moment, he didn't say a word. Then he fixed me with a wary eye.

"Do you want to replace a member of your team?"

I almost fell off my chair. "What?"

His question was so far removed from the crises on Earth that I didn't follow.

"If Thomas Warfield is a problem, you can replace him."

"At this point? Three days until launch? You have got to be kidding." So much for me remaining calm. "You can't introduce a new member into our team. Tom is essential. If he's replaced, we'd have to replace Gloria, too. No way."

"Not necessarily. Dr. Monroe would be joined to a new team member."

Appalled, I nearly leapt out of the chair. Instead, I tightened the grip on my hands. My knuckles gleamed white but didn't shake. "This isn't a game where one piece can be switched out and replaced by another. Tom and Gloria are joined as surely as if they're married. We all are. Bill and Ana. Marsh and me. That's how you and the other directors set up the teams."

He gave me an odd look. *What?* He knew we were all romantically attached. That's what the *Powers That Be* planned for all three teams. Two-by-two. Go forth and multiply. But they wouldn't let us formalize the unions. I didn't understand why. Marsh and I had talked—separately and together—to Jim and The Powers back at White Sands. We wanted to marry. Each time, they refused to grant us permission. I knew Bill and Ana had petitioned the supervisors. Tom and Gloria, too. It didn't make sense that they would send us forth to "seed" our new home and not legalize the unions.

But that wasn't the issue now.

Calm down, calm down, calm down. "I think we've gotten a little far afield. I will return to your original question. No. I do not wish to replace a member of my team. We are a unit. An efficient team."

Ashcroft sat back, relief in his eyes, in fact in his whole expression. "I'm glad to hear that."

Suspicion niggled is way into my mind. "What brought on that line of questioning?"

Sweat broke out on his upper lip. "As I mentioned before, I heard about an

28

incident yesterday. The incident apparently occurred before you declared your team required downtime. I didn't learn about it until later. Or I would have talked to you about it at the time."

"May I ask how you learned about this so-called incident?" I had a pretty good idea, but I wanted it verified.

"You may ask." His chuckle seemed forced.

I fixed my best stare on him. "Director?"

"Now, now, Sara." He was trying to placate me. After all the years we'd worked together, he should've known better. I could be relentless when necessary.

"Don't *now-now* me, Director. I'll ask again." I gripped the arms of my chair and leaned forward. "Who is spreading gossip?"

Ashcroft wiped his bald pate. He had hair, just not on top. His handkerchief mussed his graying monk's fringe. Using extreme care, he refolded his handkerchief before putting it carefully in his trouser pocket. Unlike the rest of the staff on Titan Station who wore jumpsuits, Jim still wore office attire—dark slacks, white shirt, dark striped tie.

"For the sake of harmony aboard the station, I prefer not to answer, especially now that I have your assurance no difficult situation took place." He waited, worry still in his expression.

"Director Ashcroft, my team is a cohesive unit. We are ready for the mission." I stood, ready to bolt. My team needed know what had transpired. "Is there anything else, sir?"

"No." He waved me to go. "Enjoy dinner. Dismissed."

Yeah, right. Enjoy dinner? Such a comedian. He knew what we were having for dinner tonight . . . and the rest of our meals until launch.

When I left the conference room, I almost ran into Marsh leaning against the corridor wall. He raised his eyebrow in question.

"In a minute." I couldn't talk to him about what Jim said. If someone had heard our private discussion in the lavatory, no telling who might hear it in the corridor. And report that, too.

He looked around. "Supply closet?" he whispered.

I nodded, and we headed for the closest one.

"What do you think about this latest news?" I asked as we walked.

He shook his head. "We need to get our people off the planet."

"But how? The mega-ships aren't ready. Do you think they're doing enough with the caves and bio-domes?"

"I don't know. But they'd damn well better keep their promise about taking care of our families." He opened the door to a janitor's closet.

I closed the door but held onto the handle. The stench from a nasty mop turned my stomach. I pulled the collar of my jumpsuit over my nose. Through the fabric, I told him what Jim had said. Judging from Marsh's expression, he felt the same way I did. I tapped his lips so he wouldn't explode.

"Tell the team, will you?" I whispered. "It's my exercise time, and I'm sure a certain someone is waiting there to gloat."

The door handle jiggled behind my back. When I gave Marsh a panicked glance, he wrapped his arms around my waist and kissed me. The handle jiggled again and I let go.

"What are you two—" The Weasel. "Geez. Get a room."

We broke apart. As I zipped up my jumpsuit, I said, "Hi, Erik. Need a mop?"

Marsh and I brushed past my nemesis whose mouth hung open. *Shithead.*

Leaving The Weasel behind, we headed to the habitat corridor. Exercise could wait. By unspoken agreement, we stopped at our teammates' rooms. Marsh took Bill and Ana's, while I knocked on Tom and Gloria's door.

I told them about Jim's question and my response.

Gloria, who'd been sitting at the desk, leaped up and raced over to Tom on the bed. "They can't split us up, can they? Not now."

He pulled her down next to him. "I told you before what would happen if they tried."

When she nodded, my curiosity rose. I waited for them to share. They didn't.

"Listen," I said. "It won't happen. We're a team. Nobody gets replaced."

"That's right," Marsh said behind me. "We're all going. Sara and I won't let them break up the team. We wanted you to know what happened after the meeting between Sara and Jim. No worries. But be careful."

They nodded, somewhat reassured.

After we left, I said, "Thanks. I appreciated the backup."

"Always, my love." He laid a smacking kiss on me.

"I take it Bill and Ana didn't react much."

He shook his head "They feel the same way we do. We're a team, and that's that. Off to the gym with you." He smacked me again . . . with his hand on my butt.

Remembering his earlier concern, I said, "Don't worry about your family. The Powers promised to take care of them."

He gave me a skeptical look. "How would we know they kept their promise?"

At the junction between Admin and the exercise room, we parted company. Marsh headed on through to the media room while I veered toward the gym.

I knew how important family was for him. While he rejected their lifestyle—farming—he loved them, often talking fondly about growing up in a small community where everyone knew everyone. When we learned of the tsunami, I thought how lucky they were to be so far inland. If a volcano erupted—a supervolcano, as they surmised—no one would escape the effects.

To work off my worry about what I couldn't change, I hopped onto a treadmill, deliberately choosing the one next to Erik the Weasel. How that jerk ever got this far in the training was beyond me—even if he was one of the best engineers. He'd made it clear that he should have been selected for the Primary Team, not Tom.

"Is everything all right, Grenard?" The Weasel's concern was as fake as his expression. Short and slender, like the animal we'd named him for, he must have raced here from the closet to wait for me to show up—his usual practice whenever the director called in my team.

I smiled when I really wanted to deck him. "Of course. Why do you ask?"

"Heard you had a problem yesterday."

"Really? Where did you hear that?"

A spot of red crept up his neck. "Around."

"My, my, how rumors fly. You shouldn't believe everything you hear."

I ramped up my speed and easily surpassed The Weasel. He tried to keep up and failed. That pissed him off more than my not rising to his bait. He expected me to get mad. I was, but I'd never give him the satisfaction.

Being the engineer on the Shadow Team, he *could* replace Tom. And, boy oh boy, did he want to.

Over my dead body.

We were a small community on Titan—service workers, technicians, astronauts, support staff, and Director Ashcroft, of course. I almost felt sorry for Jim. The rest of us had our teams. He had no one other than his fellow directors at Ares Station and his bosses at White Sands. Plus, he had to be worried about his family—a wife and two girls, who had to be in their teens by now. Maybe he could get them to Ares Station.

I'd read horror stories about a nuclear winter. Would the survivors react like the looters and pillagers after the tsunami? Or would they help each other? The Powers damn well better keep their promises to us. But it wasn't as if we could return and hold their feet to the fire to get them to take care of our families.

My mind wandered while I ran. From this latest crisis back to The Weasel. I'd heard rumors that his team often tried to muzzle him. I speculated that they feared he'd be responsible for their team being sent back to Ares or, worse, dismissed. Frankly, if I was the leader of that group, I'd have sent him packing right from the beginning—even if his uncle was some high up mucky-muck with UESA. I had no use for showboats or tattle-tales.

The United Earth Space Agency ran all exploration into the great unknown. A descendent of NASA, a once powerful organization that sent the first astronauts from the United States, UESA was a joint conglomerate of the myriad space agencies from all over Earth. Once individual agencies stopped vying for supremacy and worked together, space exploration flourished. Good thing. Earth was reaching critical mass with its unbridled population explosion. We were using up our resources too quickly. Since the inhabitants ignored the zero-population growth directive and refused to cease dependency on non-renewal energy sources, we either perished as a species or moved on. Add to that nature rebelling with severe climate changes, our mission had become humankind's best—only?—chance for survival.

UESA was sending teams from Earth to three Goldilocks planets—those that weren't too hot, not too cold, with an environment similar to what we were used to. My team represented the United Americas. Yuri Pushenko's represented Euro-Africa. Kaito Tanaka's team represented Asia and the Pacific Islands. Exciting and scary to hold the hopes and dreams of billions. They depended on us for survival.

And I wouldn't let The Weasel deter us.

While I thought about my responsibilities, my speed increased. The Weasel left. Finally. And I settled into my usual stride. With one hand, I picked up the VR glasses and twirled the setting until I got to the beach. Now I was running on hard-packed sand, the deep blue of the Pacific Ocean on my left. I could almost smell the salt air.

This was where I wanted to be—on a beach. The site for our landing on Serenity was within walking distance of a large lake. If I couldn't be near the ocean, a lake would do. We had such hopes for our mission. Scared and hopeful. What a combination. Three years in cryosleep. For me, the scariest part.

I forced myself not to think about all that could go wrong. So many people were depending on us. If all went well—that is, if we survived launch and cryo—one of the teams would find a planet that could be the answer to Earth's problems. Or maybe all three would. We could only hope.

I was excited and nervous. In some respects, I wished it was launch day. Just get it over with. Put me in cryosleep, where I can't think and won't dream. At least, that's what the scientists told us. I dreamed all the time. Happy dreams about Marsh, sometimes about my parents and the wonderful life they'd had together. Together was how they left this world. At the time, it was devastating, losing my parents at the same time. As grief eased, I realized how difficult it would have been for either of them to go on alone. Yet, that was how they'd left me. Alone.

Until Marsh.

Sometimes my dreams were frightening. Choking to death on the viscous substance that replaced the air in our lungs, my most frequent nightmare. Or our shuttle craft plummeting to the surface and crashing. I often woke up shaking, terrified, until Marsh put his strong arm around my waist and pulled me tight against him.

"Ah, Sara. How does it go?"

I whipped off the VR glasses. Yuri Pushenko, his royal blue jumpsuit crisp as usual, ran on the treadmill next to me. I swear the man ironed his clothes every hour. He was that fastidious.

"It goes well, Yuri." Contrary to him, I breathed heavily. "How about you?"

"I hear you have trouble." When I gave him a startled look, he laughed. "You think we are all blind and deaf?" He chuckled softly. "The snake is up to his usual tricks."

"Snake?" Comprehension dawned and I chuckled, too. "We call him The Weasel."

"Weasel? Yes, good name. He tries to sow dissention in hopes of getting on a team."

"I take it he is a problem for you, too?"

"You are not alone, golubushka."

The first time he called me that, I asked what it meant. He only smiled so I asked MT, our medical android, who knew everything. Although it literally meant *little dove*, it could mean *my darling*. I just hoped Marina, his second in command and his partner, never heard him call me that. I convinced myself he referred to our height difference. To a hulking six and a half foot tall Russian, I was little at five-six. Because my communication skills were better—according to him—than the comm specialist on his team, he'd often tried to recruit me.

His team named their future home Peace. Late one night, they decorated the outside of their ship with symbols of peace—a dove with an olive branch in its beak plus the old peace sign. Later, the Japanese team painted a crane for good luck on all three ships.

Since the plan for our team was to land on Serenity on Christmas Day, we painted a wreath on one side and a radiating star on the other. The directors were not pleased at the artistic efforts. They said we desecrated the ships. But they didn't order us to paint over the symbols.

I thought about what Yuri had revealed. "Has The Weasel done anything to your team?"

"He tried." His deep laugh came from his belly. "Milos threatened to snip something vital, and The Snake backed off. I am surprised he has waited this long to work against you."

"Not the first time." I blew out a disgusted breath. Not one I could afford, either. Breathing heavily, I needed to start my cool down. "I thought it was just us, since he's from the Americas."

"He is desperate." Yuri increased his speed, faster than mine at my peak. "Are you finished running already?"

I was walking now but definitely finished. I threw him a wry grin. "What do you mean already? I ran from LA to San Francisco today." A slight exaggeration.

Yuri threw his head back and laughed. "Me, I run from Moscow to Kiev."

He made me smile, and for a moment I forgot about The Weasel and Director Ashcroft and Earth's crises. When my machine came to a stop, I hopped off and picked up my towel.

"Sara?" His serious tone stopped me from leaving.

"He is frightened. And desperate. Do not allow him to disconcert you."

"Ri-ight. Easier said than done."

"I know. You will be fine. Your team is ready. As is mine." He grinned broadly.

Heartened by his words, I called out, "Have fun on your walk to Kiev." I waved then left the exercise room.

I knew we couldn't let Erik and his tricks get to us. Just three more days. As our fears increased, tension rose. We'd done well up to this point. We couldn't blow it now. Not after four years.

How quickly those years had flown by. We had been at the training center near White Sands, New Mexico when the first crisis hit. They sent the teams to Mars, escalated the training, then this last year on Titan. At the beginning, looking ahead often made me groan. Eight long years. That had been the plan. Not for our three teams, though. We got half that. The other teams would get more training at a slower pace. Lucky them.

Or not. Here we were. Only three days left. The hopes of humankind weighing heavily on our shoulders.

On my way to my quarters, I stopped in a restroom. As soon as I pushed open the door, Gloria and one of the girls from the Shadow Team broke apart. Gloria, our team physician who had the most sympathetic ear, had been holding Sharlene. A red-faced, teary-eyed Sharlene.

"Sorry." I started to back out, but Sharlene shook her head.

"I'm leaving." Her voice sounded thick with tears.

Gloria gave her a hug and said, "It will all work out. Have faith."

After Sharlene left, Gloria slumped against a sink. "Shit, shit, shit."

She never swore. She often turned into a tyrant when any of us used foul language.

"Are you okay?" I knew she wasn't. I tried not to pry into my crew's personal life, but this was my best friend. Different rules.

"That goddamn piece of wormwooded shithead son of a bitch." With each nasty name, she pounded the top of her thigh. She went on with a litany of name calling my mother would have washed my mouth out for saying.

When she wound down, I said, "Are you going to tell me who? On second thought, if it's one of our team, I don't want to know."

Gloria shook her head. "Not our team. The Weasel."

"What did he do now?" I headed toward the row of sinks. I wanted a shower but was more interested in what Gloria had to say about Erik the Weasel. As I washed my hands then splashed water on my face, I said, "By the way, I had a chat with Yuri Pushenko. Did you know they call him The Snake? I didn't realize he's been—"

"She's pregnant."

Gloria's pronouncement stopped me cold. Water dripped off my face and down my shirt. "What! Who?"

She looked around, as if someone had come in since I did. I waited. Gloria grabbed a hand towel then came closer. "Sharlene," she whispered as she handed me the towel.

"How?" I clunked my head against the mirror above the sink. Duh.

For the past year, all of us on the primary teams had been forbidden to have intercourse. No one, not even the scientists, knew the effect of cryo on an embryo or fetus. Even before that, I insisted Marsh and I refrain. Despite scientific advances, birth control was still not one hundred percent effective. The ban included the Shadow Team.

"He told her he hated condoms, and since she was taking preventive measures, he didn't need to use anything."

"Idiot." I blotted my face. "How could he be so stupid? And why did she let him?"

Gloria pursed her lips. "Is that really important? As soon as Ashcroft finds out, she's off the team."

That sobered me up. "No wonder she was crying."

"She told The Weasel, of course. He said it was her problem. Shithead." Gloria snorted. "That isn't a strong enough name. She came to me and asked if I could check her out to be sure."

"Did you?"

Gloria nodded. "Nothing like doing an exam while the patient is lying on a narrow bench." Her mouth quirked up. "I locked the door, of course. I'd just unlocked it when she started bawling again."

"What's going to happen now?"

"She'll be sent home."

That hit me hard. That could have been me, if Marsh and I had gone against the dictate. Pregnancy would have taken me out of the program. As much as I wanted a child, being commander of this mission was more important. Besides, I had no home to return to. I'd sold off everything before leaving for Ares Station on Mars and put the proceeds into a scholarship trust in memory of my parents. Despite that bad incident, bright kids attended my old high school. Kids who needed assistance. I hoped they appreciated the sacrifice I made for them.

Washing out of the program wasn't an option for me. Neither was going back to my old life. If necessary, I guess, I would've found a way. Sharlene was likable and brilliant. She would find a way, too. Unfortunately, she'd have to give up her dream to satisfy a selfish jerk.

"I know you won't tell anyone," Gloria said. "Besides Marsh. I know you. You share everything with him."

I nodded. "I wouldn't keep something like that from him. I'll be discreet. Sharlene has to deal with the director. I wouldn't force her." I snapped my fingers. "That's why that jerk tattled to Ashcroft about Tom and Marsh. With Sharlene gone, he won't have a partner. He's trying to weasel his way onto our team."

She gave me a droll look. "*Weasel* his way?"

"Pun intended."

"You are so bad. We'd better be careful. He's desperate. He'll do anything to take out one of the guys." She clapped her hand over her mouth. "If he got Tom kicked off the team, he'd be—" Her face paled. "—my partner." She pretended to gag.

"Not to worry. I won't let that happen." I patted her shoulder. "I need a shower."

She wrinkled her nose. "You sure do. Don't let me stop you."

"I need to get some clean clothes."

She stopped me from heading for the door. "Take your shower. I'll set your clothes on the bench."

That was Gloria. Always looking after us. A true mother hen. She would make a wonderful mother when we finally got to Serenity.

I let the shower wash away the stink from exercising and also my thoughts. What if I broke my arm/foot/leg before liftoff? I couldn't imagine watching my team—the people I'd come to love as a family—leave without me. I had to be more vigilant, more cautious. I could even slip in the shower. Gingerly, I stepped out of the shower and reached for my towel.

Marsh handed it to me. "I ran into Gloria. She gave me your clothes." He pointed to the bench.

He had his back to the door, shielding me from the sight of anyone who might walk in. I'd say what a gentleman, but not the way he ogled me. I looped my arms around his neck and plastered my naked body against him.

After a quick hug, he gave me a long, speculative look then wrapped the towel around my torso. When he tucked an end into the top, he made sure to graze my breasts.

"Not nice." My giggle negated my little reprimand.

"I wondered if you were going to run until tomorrow."

I grinned. "Yuri and I were running to Kiev."

"All the way from San Francisco?"

"Nope. Just from Carmel." I finished dressing. "After everything that's gone on, I need another hug."

He obliged me. "Oh, hey. We could do this—"

After glancing toward the door, I bit his ear. "Let's go back to our room," I whispered. "I have more to tell you."

Marsh tried to back away, but I held onto his neck. Again, I whispered, "We don't want to give that nosy parker more ammunition." Out loud, I said, "Kiss me again, Marsh. I just love it when you—"

He covered my mouth, cutting me off. When he came up for air, he said, "I love your kisses, too, Sara mine. Let's move this to our quarters."

After he opened the door, I checked the corridor. A shadow disappeared around the corner at the end of the hall. Someone had been listening at the door. I was sure of it. I was also sure of who it was.

"What did Yuri want?" Marsh asked.

"Commiserating about a mutual problem."

When Marsh pulled me down the hall to our quarters, I ran on my toes. I hadn't taken time to put on my shoes. In bed, he wanted to make love while I wanted to tell him about my news. Not that I didn't want to make love, mind you. But despite my running on the treadmill, I was still steamed about the snaky Weasel. Ooh, I loved that. Mixing up the Russian and our designation for the creep.

As I laid my head on his pillow, my mouth next to his ear, I whispered, telling him about Sharlene.

"That son of a bitch." He reared up.

I didn't have to warn him not to tell anyone about Sharlene and The Weasel. Marsh was a vault. Once something went in, it took a pry bar to get it out.

"Ah. That's why you were gone so long. And I thought you were being virtuous and exercising."

"Do you want me to be virtuous?"

"No." He nuzzled my neck.

"I saw The Weasel in the exercise room," he whispered into my ear. "Did he say anything?"

"Of course. I didn't give him the satisfaction of a response. But then I didn't know about his partner. If we weren't so close to the launch, I'd bust his chops."

"Glad you didn't. You'd probably break your hand, and they'd have to replace you." He sucked on the tender skin below my ear.

I growled and bit his chin. "You are never replacing me."

He climbed on top of me. "Enough talk. Let's do it before we have to go to dinner."

Groaning, I looped my arms around his neck. "Tonight's the night, right?"

He balanced himself over me. As he slid down my body, nibbling along the way, he mused, "Hmm. Mushroom-covered steak. A baked potato swimming in butter, coconut cream pie for—"

I swatted him. "Cruel."

MT held out an IV needle. "Good evening, Commander. Diet Coke coming up." She winked.

"Don't I wish."

An hour earlier, the med team inserted ports in our arms where we would take our meals via IV infusion. Whatever was in the bag hanging from the pole attached to my chair was supposed to give me all the nutrients my body needed. Hah. I'd rather have real food. Tomorrow came the real fun when they evacuated all wastes from our bodies. Couldn't have anything in our gastro-intestinal tracks when we went into cryosleep. I thought of the best meals I'd ever had and pretended that was coursing through my veins.

Why was it when you couldn't have something, you craved it?

My reverie about Mom's lasagna and homemade cannoli came to an abrupt halt when Marsh pulled out his chair.

He held his arm out to MT. "Sock it to me."

She chuckled. "May I interest you in a nice Cabernet Sauvignon?" She slipped the needle into the port in Marsh's left arm.

"Yes, that will go nicely with tonight's special. Beef Wellington, right?"

"Sick, buddy. Real sick." Tom held out Gloria's chair on my right.

"Hey, Tommy boy," Bill said. He and Ana already had their IVs attached. "Lighten up. I'm having Kansas City's best barbeque. Ana here's having a Maine lobster."

She whapped his good arm. "I'm vegetarian or have you forgotten?"

He laid a smacking kiss on her that left Ana sputtering. He grinned. "If we can't joke about our situation, we're in bad shape."

Yuri's team sat at a round table a short distance away. He raised his water glass to me then to Kaito. I smiled and raised mine to them.

"What are you guys having?" Bill called to the other teams. "We're having barbeque."

Yuri chuckled. "Veal Orlov. And, of course, caviar."

Kaito looked slightly confused then smiled. "Toshikoshi soba. For New Year's Eve. And Ishikari nabe, a hot pot." He mimicked using chopsticks to transfer food to his non-existent plate.

The others—staff, technicians—stared at us as if we were a little crazy.

"Enough. All this talk about food is making me even more hungry," I said before trying to change the subject. "Has anyone heard the football scores?"

We chatted about the chances of our favorite teams getting into the Super Bowl. I took a small sip of water, the only fluid we were allowed. Considering the full bag of liquid nutrients, I'd better go easy on the water, or I'd be up all night peeing.

The hair on the back of my neck prickled. I looked around. Across the dining room, I noticed The Weasel staring at me. Sharlene was nowhere in sight.

T minus two days and counting

I hurried into the lav after Tom, who'd abruptly left our team meeting. If I wasn't mistaken, the others were right behind me. Tom was hugging a toilet and retching.

Gloria grabbed a washcloth from the linen cupboard and soaked it. She knelt beside him and wiped his face. We all knew advanced first aid—requisite training—but we stood back and let the doctor administer aid and comfort. A lot more of the latter, since Tom was her partner.

"Did you snitch something to eat?" Gloria asked.

"I didn't," he muttered. "I swear."

Marsh and I looked at each other. Despite Tom's lanky appearance, he had a voracious appetite. His late night forays to the kitchen were legendary. I wouldn't have put it past him to ease his empty stomach with a little solid nourishment despite all the warnings from the medical staff.

"Nerves?" Bill asked.

Not an unreasonable explanation. The closer we got to the launch, the more uptight everyone became, myself included. My stomach had been in knots since early that morning, partially because of anticipation. Since yesterday's meeting with Ashcroft, I was more worried that something might happen to disrupt our team. They wouldn't delay the launch. We had a tight window when everything lined up. That was why we had a backup team.

Wished I could be around when it was their turn, and they had a Shadow Team that hoped they'd screw up. Unfortunately, my wish could only come true if I were bumped from my team.

"Honest, guys," Tom said weakly. "Only water at lunch."

Ana came through the door. I never even saw her leave. I needed to keep my mind from wandering. Tom was still sitting on the floor, but he leaned back against the wall of the stall. Gloria squatted next to him, her blonde hair brushing against his sweat-mussed dark head. She held the cloth against his forehead.

"This will help." Ana held out a cup of dark liquid. "Small sips."

"We're not supposed to—"

She glared at me. Ana was our food specialist and a world-class herbologist. Her knowledge of plants surpassed all of ours, even though we received training on recognizing edible and poisonous flora.

Redundancy was the byword for every skill. We trained in multi-disciplines in the hopefully rare event that the specialist became disabled.

The door hit Bill in the back. He spun around, blocking the small opening with his foot. "Go somewhere else," he said. "We're having a meeting."

The Weasel whined that he needed to go. Bill slammed the door in his face and locked it.

"Sorry, guys." Bill grimaced. "I should have done that as soon as Ana returned."

Again, Marsh looked at me. From his raised eyebrow, I knew he was thinking the same thing I was. The Weasel did something to Tom and had come to check out the results.

"How are you feeling?" I asked.

Tom gave me a weak smile. "I'll live."

"Good thing." I smiled back. "Can't have you upchucking in your helmet during launch."

Bill made a face. "Thank you, Commander, for that image."

"Always glad to help."

As Tom struggled to his feet, Gloria tucked her shoulder under his arm. He seemed steady. For a moment. Then he slid down to the floor.

Not good.

"If we support him while getting him to his quarters," Marsh said, "they'll know something is wrong."

"He should be examined by the medical staff," I said, even though that was the last thing I wanted.

"No."

That was unanimous. All five voices responded at once.

"Suggestions?" I looked around at each person. "We need to get him out of here before the director comes to investigate. You know The Weasel will tell him we're hogging the restroom."

"We can rig up a litter," Marsh said. "Bill, check the supply closet for two brooms. Ana, find a blanket."

As they did his bidding, I leaned close to him. "And how do we explain why we're carrying Tom on a litter?"

Marsh smiled. "Leave the explanations to me. Hang on. Just thought of something." He went to the linen closet and returned with a sheet. Using his pocketknife, he slit the hem then tore the sheet into strips. "One around Tom's head and one around his forearm."

I could see where he was going with that. I grabbed one of the strips and wrapped it around Tom's head, while Bill wrapped another around Tom's leg, and Ana took care of his arm.

"What are you guys doing to me? It's my belly that's the problem."

"Oh, hush," I said. "Play along."

Between us, we got Tom on a make-shift litter. As we carefully lifted him, someone pounded on the door.

"What is going on in there?" Director Ashcroft. "Open the door immediately."

Ana, who was the smallest, let go of the litter. She opened the door.

"What are you people—" Ashcroft stopped and gaped at us. "What—"

"Isn't it obvious, sir?" Marsh said. "We're practicing field conditions. If you'll step aside, we'll get this man to our med unit." He winked at the director. "That's his quarters."

"Commander?" Ashcroft looked pointedly at me.

"Sir, may we pass?" I said. "This man needs to be in the med unit where Dr. Monroe can examine his wounds more thoroughly. Marsh can explain this scenario on the way."

With Marsh and Bill at Tom's head, Gloria and me at his feet, and Ana leading the way to open doors, we carried him out of the lav. Several people gawked at us as we passed them in hall. The Weasel's mouth dropped. I wanted to smash his chin closed.

"Director," Marsh said as we walked down the hall toward our quarters. "In this scenario, Bill and Tom were cutting down a dead tree for firewood. The tree didn't land where they planned. Instead, it fell on Tom. As you can see, we used what we had on hand—those aren't really brooms. They're tree branches."

"Interesting," Ashcroft admitted. "It would have been helpful to advise me of this *practice scenario*."

"Well, sir," Marsh said. "It was a spontaneous exercise. Sara has been coming up with different scenarios to test our ability to think on our feet. So to speak."

"This has really helped our ability to handle situations your team hasn't thought of," Gloria added. "In this instance, Bill had to do basic first aid while waiting for the rest of us to show up. We developed shortcut codes to summon the team via our comm units." She held up one arm with a pretend comm around her wrist.

Ashcroft looked at Tom. "What do you think of being a victim, Warfield?"

Before Tom could speak, Gloria said, "Sir, he's delirious. We cautioned him to save his strength and keep quiet."

"Director," Bill continued, "we've learned how to use resources at hand. In a previous exercise Sara devised, we simulated being lost. Ana—"

"I get the picture." Ashcroft didn't look convinced.

When we arrived at Tom's quarters, Ana held the door. "This is our med unit, Director. If you'll step aside, we'll put Tom on the regen bed and let the machine do its job."

Ashcroft backed away. "Very inventive. Carry on. Commander, give me a list of the scenarios my team missed. That will be useful for future teams."

I nodded just before Ana closed and locked the door, keeping the entourage of onlookers at bay. Gently, we laid Tom on his bed, but Marsh cautioned us not to unwrap our make-shift bandages from his head, arm, and leg. Gloria plunged into doctor mode, issuing whispered orders to the rest of us.

"Let's extend this exercise." She glanced toward the door, as if surmising someone might continue to eavesdrop on our simulation game. She must have also thought about the monitor minions. All we'd need was for one of them to report back to Ashcroft. "With an injured leg, he'll need assistance to the lav. Bill, Marsh, give him a hand. Tom, we want this to be authentic. Lean on them as if you can't stand on your leg."

Tom gave her a grateful look while Marsh and Bill assisted him to his feet.

"Come on, team," I said. "We'll critique this scenario in the lav."

As I checked the corridor, once again I saw a shadow at the end, as if someone just disappeared around the corner. Good thing we'd stayed in exercise mode. Even though the lav was for our team's use only, I locked the door behind us. No more sneaky weasels hanging around, listening. I hoped.

The guys led Tom to the bench farthest from the door.

"Thanks for covering for me," he whispered. "I don't know what I'd do if they knocked me off the team." His hang-dog expression made Gloria rub his shoulder while Ana hovered close by.

We all knew how he felt. Each of us would feel the same way if we were in his situation. After four years of training, of anticipating, I would be devastated if I were left behind.

However, I had to think of the welfare of the team and of Tom in particular. "If you're not better in four hours, I'll have to go to the director."

"You can't," Gloria cried.

"We may not have a choice," Marsh interrupted. "Sara's right. We can't risk Tom's life. What if he has a serious medical condition?"

Bill nodded. "I hate to admit this, but Marsh's real time scenario has merit." He patted Tom's shoulder. "Listen, old buddy, you need to get better in four hours. Who's going to keep me on the straight and narrow if you're not there?"

"Thanks, guys." Tom spoke through clenched teeth. "Ana, got any more of that magic elixir?"

She pulled a flask out of the inside of her belted jumpsuit. I'd noticed how blousy it was but attributed it to the exertion of carrying Tom. "Good job, Ana, hiding that from the director and those lookee-loos."

Tom took small sips then leaned against the wall. Color slowly came back into his face. Fortunately, Ashcroft hadn't noticed how wan Tom looked earlier. Or maybe he had and chose not to ask. That was taking playacting to the max.

A half hour later, we trooped out of the lav one by one, with Tom sandwiched between Marsh and Bill. I was the last one out, eager to see how they managed. Marsh waited outside our room, a grin creasing his face. He gave me a small thumbs-up before heading down the corridor. Part of me wanted to follow. It was his workout time. Another part of me needed a nap.

The latter won.

As I lay on my bed, forearm across my eyes, I reflected on how we'd dodged a potentially disastrous situation. Tom looked better. I knew Gloria would take care of him. If only there was a way to prove The Weasel tried to sabotage our team.

"Hey, wake up, sleepyhead," Marsh called softly. "Time for dinner. I hear grilled mahi-mahi with pineapple chutney is the main course."

"That is not funny." I groaned and rolled away.

"With tiramisu for dessert," he said in singsong fashion.

"You are a cruel man, Marsh Rayburn." I staggered to the small sink against the wall then splashed water on my face. I didn't realize I'd fallen asleep. One look in the mirror, and I saw that I had a serious case of bedhead.

"C'mon, sweetheart," he said. "Don't be such a grump."

How could he be so blasé about our last meals until we reached Serenity?

T minus one day and counting

It was our last Christmas in civilization. That evening, we celebrated with the other teams. A party that combined Earth's December celebrations—Christmas, Chanukah, Kwanzaa, Mawlid an-Nabī, Dhanu Sankranti, Bodhi Day, even Omisoka because none of us would be here for New Year's Eve. Secular symbols made sure those who didn't follow a religion weren't left out.

I watched my team, as well as the other two. The Shadow Team had not been invited. Just the eighteen of us who were to embark on an epic journey. The laughter was a little too loud. The gaiety forced, not aided by alcohol that we couldn't have. We mingled, chatted about irrelevant topics. None of us broached the crises on Earth. Or our responsibility to save the world we knew.

Yuri and Kaito cornered me near a viewport.

"What do you think, Sara-san?" Kaito's black eyes twinkled. "Does your team have the Right Stuff?"

I chuckled. "You bet. And yours?"

"But of course."

Yuri's belly laugh made me smile. "Neither of you have as great a team as I. We will reach our new home first, even if Sara has a head start."

"Whoa. My planet is farthest away."

"Yours is closest, Yuri," Kaito said. "It is only fair you go last."

"That means we will get there first." Yuri smirked.

Kaito and I shared a look. Neither of us could walk away from a challenge. I said, "Since there are too many variables not under our control, how's this for a challenge? The first team that completes a permanent settlement in the shortest amount of time after landing wins."

We negotiated the terms—what exactly the settlement contained, how many buildings, etc. Then we laid our hands on top of the others' to seal the pact.

"What are you three conspiring?" Marsh put his hands on my shoulders. Though I wasn't fond of public displays of affection, I didn't mind his touch. Until he rubbed his thumbs across the tops of my arms. My face warmed. Considering the looks from the other men, they knew exactly what Marsh was doing to me.

"It looks like the party is breaking up," Yuri observed. "Better to continue in private."

Marsh dropped his hands.

Diane Burton

As Yuri passed, he said, "Be careful, golubushka." He patted my shoulder then looked at Marsh. "Watch her back."

"Always."

Kaito gave me a short bow. "An honor, Sara-san. Be most careful."

I returned his bow. "You, too."

Marsh sprawled beside me. As usual, he took up three-quarters of the bed. All relaxed, snoring loud enough to wake the dead, the hard planes of his face softened in sleep. I'd say he slept like a baby if that wasn't such a cliché. He slept like he didn't have a care in the world, as if he wasn't going to be crammed into a tube tomorrow and turned into a humongous ice cube for three years.

I, on the other hand, hadn't even closed my eyes since we turned out the lights. Fear slithered through my consciousness. FEAR in capital letters. Despite all the simulations, despite the training, even though I calmly accepted our mission, I was terrified.

Too late to back out now.

As if I would.

Excitement and wonder pushed down the fear. I reminded myself that out of the hundreds of thousands of applicants, I was chosen to lead our team on the adventure of a lifetime. That the people of Earth depended on us.

All was quiet on Titan Station. Everything was ready for the first explorations beyond our solar system. Tomorrow. Like other early explorers on Earth, who had no idea where they were going yet sailed off anyway, we didn't know what we'd find.

Oh, yes, we'd seen hi-rez pictures from the probes. The terrain of Serenity was imprinted on my brain. I knew every meter within a hundred kilometers around LZ-1, our home-away-from-home for the rest of our lives.

The rest of my life. My breath caught in my throat. I would never return to Earth. Never see my friends again. Admittedly, I had few left. Just one of the casualties of four years of intensive training for the biggest adventure of my life. We tried to keep in touch via vid phone, but gradually we didn't make the effort—me more than them. My friends thought I was "just plain crazy." We grew apart. If my parents had still been alive, my decision to never see them again would have been more difficult. As an only child, I couldn't leave them. It was their fatal accident that propelled me into applying.

Again, my breath caught. This time on a stifled sob.

"Hey, babe." Marsh rolled toward me and threw his arm around my waist. "My God, you're strung tighter than a torsion spring." He snuggled in, nuzzling my neck. "I can help you relax."

In the dim light of our quarters, I saw him grin. "We can't. You know that. The rules—"

"Screw the rules." He tucked me under him then slid his warm hands under my T-shirt. "Hmm. I think I'd rather screw you."

"That is crude." I pushed against his big shoulders. It was like trying to push a concrete wall.

"But correct." He chuckled.

"I can't take the chance of getting pregnant. You know that."

"We can manage. We have before," he reminded me.

Yes, we had. I tried to stifle my grin. We'd been inventive—or so we imagined—in ways to give each other pleasure.

As he covered my breast, I whimpered. I wanted him, but I didn't dare. "They are watching us," I whispered.

"That's never stopped you before."

He was right. Somehow tonight was different.

"Please, Marsh. Not tonight."

With an exasperated sigh, he rolled off. "What? You have a headache?"

I turned on my side to face him. I stroked his cheek. "Don't ruin our last night together by arguing."

"Oh, Sara mine. You know I'll do anything for you." He traced my nose, my lips, my chin.

"I wish I had known you before *this*." He traced the scar under my chin, a souvenir from my high school attacker.

"It's ugly. I know." I tucked my chin down.

He lifted it up. "That is not what I meant. You wouldn't have ever needed to fear the imbecile. I would've taken care of him." He sounded deathly quiet.

That was Marsh. So good to me, taking care of me in ways I never imagined. Sacrificing his own needs for me.

"Talk to me. Keep the nightmares at bay."

"That's a pretty tall order, lady. What should I talk about?" He skimmed his fingers along my side, not light enough to tickle but not sensual enough to entice me to throw caution out the non-existent window in our small bedroom.

"Tell me why you volunteered for the mission."

He lay back on his pillow with a snort. "I've told you at least four times. You know why."

"Tell me again," I pleaded.

With a long-suffering sigh, he said, "I'm not a farmer, like my dad and brothers. They resented that I became a SEAL."

"Hang on. You skipped over the part where you joined the Navy to see the world."

"I was cutting to the chase."

"Not tonight. I want to hear everything again."

"You won't get any sleep."

"Who cares? I'm going to sleep for three years. And after tonight, I won't hear your voice until we're in Serenity's orbit."

So he told me everything again. Leaving home against his father's orders, joining the Navy, SERE training.

"Tell me again what SERE stands for?"

"Survival. Evasion. Resistance. Escape." He rubbed the top of my head with his knuckles. "You know that."

I did. His SERE experience, especially survival, would aid us on our new planet. But I wanted him to keep talking.

"Tell me more about your family." Technically, they would be my family tomorrow. But I would only know them through Marsh. We would leave a message for them before launch, just as I would leave a message for my former best friend. Not only had we grown apart, she'd written me off long ago, never understanding my need to leave Earth.

My eyes closed as I listened to him describe his family. Farmers and farmers' wives. Content to work in the nation's Breadbasket and feed the world. They knew about Marsh's mission but didn't understand that in his own way he was trying to save them. Save all of Earth's inhabitants by finding a new world. One we hadn't screwed up yet.

When his voice trailed off, I yawned widely. "I love you, Marsh."

He kissed me deeply. "Ditto, Sara." Then he held me, pushing away my fears, his big body giving the comfort I so desperately needed.

T minus six hours and counting

Morning came. At the wake-up call from Control, we became all business, going through routines. While Marsh lolled in the shower—his last for the next three years—I dressed in my one-piece jumpsuit. I wanted to wait for him, but my stomach kept growling. I needed sustenance, even if it only went into my vein. I stumbled to the mess. There I joined Gloria and Tom at our table. Yuri's and Kaito's teams hadn't arrived yet. The techs and Mission Control specialists across the room glanced up then returned to their breakfasts. Was that sympathy in their eyes? Knowing that we would never return, were they fearful? Although it would take nearly a year back to Earth, they could all go home . . . if they wanted to.

"Where's my coffee?" I held out my arm to MT.

"Hehe, Commander." The android prepared my port for the IV bag. "What else can I get you for breakfast? Eggs, pancakes, French toast?"

I was still amazed at how quickly she'd caught on to our joking.

"How about scrambled eggs, bacon well done, hash browns, and whole wheat toast?" I asked with the straightest expression I could manage.

"Coming right up."

Gloria glared at both of us as she adjusted the IV in her arm. "Sadist."

Tom just chuckled. He looked like he was feeling better. According to Gloria late yesterday, he'd had no more episodes. Thank God, I didn't have to report the incident.

"I'm having Huevos Rancheros and chorizo." He held up his glass of water. "And I'm on my second glass of fresh-squeezed orange juice."

"You are both sick," Gloria said. From the dark smudges under her eyes, I imagined she got as much sleep as I did.

Marsh stood in the doorway. "When we get to Serenity, I'm having prime rib."

Tom arched his eyebrow. "Ana says there's no beef on Serenity."

She knew best. As our flora and fauna expert, she'd examined the pictures more intently than I had.

"You do know our food will be freeze-dried," Tom added. "Until us hunters find the real stuff." He raised his arms, muscle-man style.

Marsh laughed. "Spoilsport. All of you."

He sauntered around the table with that long-legged stride of his. It was the first thing I noticed about him when we began training. Something about his easy loose-limbed walk made me pick him out of the hundreds of trainees gathered that first day. Well, his stride *and* his tight butt.

After flipping the chair around, he easily straddled it then held out his arm. "Fill 'er up, MT."

She giggled. "Aye, aye, sir."

Ana and Bill rushed in, he was grinning while she was flushed and embarrassed. Guessing what made them late, I looked away. Marsh scooted his chair closer to mine and whispered, "Told you we had time."

Now *I* was flushed and embarrassed.

The six of us chatted about inane things, no one broaching the topic uppermost in our minds. The mission. Soon, MT removed the IVs but not the ports. We would need them in cryo.

Ashcroft strode in, glanced at us then headed over to our table. "Commander Grenard, is your team ready?"

I stood. "Absolutely, sir."

He eyed us individually. "If anyone wishes to drop out, now is the time."

As if we would.

Tom snorted. Bill rolled his eyes.

After several moments of silence, Marsh stood. "On behalf of the team, I can say we are ready to go." He raised a glass of water—the most potent drink possible. "To Serenity. Our new home."

The rest of my team stood. We all raised our glasses. "Our new home," we echoed.

"The officials are waiting for you in the conference room." Ashcroft nodded before moving on to the table gradually filling up with the Asian team.

"Let's do it, folks." Marsh grinned.

Bill hummed the Wedding March. His "bum, bum-ba-dum" serenaded us down the corridor to the conference room. There a chaplain waited for us. My heart sped up. As I stood next to Marsh, squeezing his hand as if it were a lifeline, I felt more trepidation for this ceremony than for the mission.

"Do you, Sara Ann Grenard . . ."

After the six of us said our vows, signed the marriage licenses, and completed all the formalities, we each made our final videos to our families and friends. Although the transmission would take hours to reach them, Marsh and I grinned as we told his family about our marriage ceremony. He squeezed my hand and raised it so they could see both our rings.

"We will send messages as we can," he said. "May the Good Lord keep you all safe."

I heard the tears in his throat. To say good-bye to your family forever was so hard. At least, he got to say it while they were still alive. I hadn't had that luxury. I'd said my good-by to my parents at a funeral home.

I'm not a real religious person, but I believed my folks knew what I was doing, that they were adding their prayers to mine and sending them on to the Almighty. Prayers that we would have a safe trip and a flawless landing on Earth's new home.

Finally, we were herded through one last examination and inspection. I had no modesty left. I found it ironic that MT, the only non-human, treated us the most reverently. On the other hand, most of the medical team acted like we were more specimens than people. But a few had tears glistening in their eyes as they hugged us and wished us a safe journey.

Since MT would be traveling to Serenity with us, she grinned, and her eyes twinkled in anticipation. As much as I understood her excitement, in my anxious condition, I wanted to slap her.

And then it was time to board our ship, our home for the next three years.

T minus two hours

The other teams came to see us off. Yuri and Kaito gave a short speech wishing us well. I did the same. Kaito reminded us of our challenge, and Yuri bet his team would win. Director Ashcroft shook his head at our teasing. After his message and one from the head of UESA, the president of the United Earth Nations spoke directly to us. Obviously, the last two speeches had been prepared well in advance so they could be delivered before we left.

Though she didn't refer to the crises on Earth, the president ended with, "You are Earth's hope. You are our salvation."

No pressure there.

Hugs all around, then we were on our way to the launch pad. As we walked through the tunnel connecting the habitat with the launch site a kilometer away, the butterflies in my stomach began the Macarena. The closer we got to our destination, the faster the dance. Now those damn butterflies were doing a salsa. Thank goodness, I had no food in my stomach. Or my gut, for that matter.

"How ya doing?" Marsh slung her arm around my shoulder. "Feel like you're going to hurl?"

I gave him a sharp glance. "Don't talk about it."

"Everything will be all right, Sara love. We're going to make history."

The techs helped us suit up. Before we knew it, they led us to the elevator that would take us up to the command module. I gripped the bar behind me to quell my fears. I'd rather squeeze Marsh's hand and receive an answering squeeze. Maybe it was better I didn't. I'd probably crush his fingers.

T minus 5 minutes

As the control team read out stats, weather conditions, and so on, things we had no control over, I noticed Ana drumming her fingers on her arm rest. Gloria's foot tapped the floor. I worked hard to not let my nervousness show.

But Marsh knew me. Too well, I think. He said, "It will be all right, kids. We're about to join all the explorers who went before us. Magellan, Columbus, Perry, Shepard, Armstrong." He added Forester, who first landed on Mars, and Vizinsky, the first to land on Titan. So many brave adventurers.

Liftoff went well, each of us performing our assigned duties. Never mind our onboard computer could have done it all. Control wanted us to feel essential, useful. We would be . . . in three years.

Some jokers at Mission Control had christened our onboard computer "Hal"— like the computer in *2001: A Space Odyssey*. The six of us were not amused. The thought of a computer that could end our lives terrified us all, though we never let on to the jokesters.

After setting course and turning control over to Hal, I stood and faced the others. "Okay, guys, it's time. Serenity, here we come."

We hugged each other, our last human contact for three years. Gloria clung to me. When she pulled away, her eyes swam with tears. She wasn't the only one. Even reserved Ana struggled to hold back emotion. Tom and Bill turned away. Men. What was so wrong with showing how they felt?

Marsh, as second in command, stood with me as we watched our team climb into their respective tubes. MT attached wires and hoses, checked vital signs, then closed the lids and started the cryo process.

She turned to Marsh. Too soon, I wanted to shout. Instead, I hugged him tightly.

"See ya soon, kiddo." Despite his lopsided grin that always melted my heart, his eyes looked suspiciously red. My macho guy, Survivor Man, felt emotions as much as I did. He just didn't show it. Until now. "Dream of me, babe."

According to the scientists, there was no dreaming in cryo. He knew that. But I replied, "Only if you dream of me." I kissed him soundly then stepped back.

As he unzipped his jumpsuit, he winked at me then shimmied in a mock striptease. He even hummed "The Stripper" as he did to me in our quarters. Beneath his suit, he wore a skin-tight brief that I swear was smaller than a Speedo. I was no prude, but Marsh's scrap of material was so formfitting I felt myself getting hot.

"Feast your eyes on this." He posed, strong-man style, turning this way and that until MT tsked and chivvied him into his tube that looked like a coffin.

I wished I hadn't thought that.

Too soon, way too soon, MT closed his lid, started the process, then looked at me. "Your turn, Commander."

I peered at Marsh through the round window of his cryotube. His eyes were already closed. I kissed my fingertips then laid them on the window. One last kiss for my love. "See you on Christmas," I whispered.

We would celebrate Christmas Day 2175 in our new home. On Serenity.

MT led me to my tube. She helped me out of my jumpsuit. Like the other women, I wore a white unitard to preserve my modesty. As if I had any left after all the examinations. But when I thought of the cameras filming and techs watching, anything that covered my body was okay with me.

"Ready to turn into a popsicle, Commander?" MT grinned then waited patiently as I gave the tubes lined along the bulkhead another look.

"I guess so." I straightened my shoulders. "Scratch that. I am ready." As I'd done several times before, I climbed inside. The simulations supposedly prepared us for this moment. Real Time was definitely not the same.

"Commander, your heartrate is going whacko."

"Whacko is not a medical term." Hal's voice came from the speaker on the far wall. "You must use proper medical terminology."

"Hah! What do you know? My methods—and my terminology—are just fine. Think good thoughts, Commander." When I thought about Marsh, MT said, "Whatever you're thinking about, stop it."

"But you told me—"

"Your estrogen levels are climbing sky-high."

Oh, boy. Wouldn't the monitor minions enjoy that! Damn voyeurs.

"Her vital signs are spiking," Hal reported. "Make her control them."

"Yeah right, you hunk of junk. She won't settle down if we're arguing. You know the Commander. She'll try to negotiate a peace settlement between us." MT leaned close to my ear. "Please settle down, Commander, or we'll never hear the end of his griping."

I forced myself to think about walking on the beach. Okay, I felt my heart slow down. I wouldn't think about Marsh and what I wanted to do with him after we landed.

"Really, Commander?" MT gave me a smug look. "The others didn't give me half the problems you are. Settle down. Think good thoughts," she repeated.

Sitting on the sand, warmed by the day's sun. Watching that sun descend until it disappeared into the ocean. Listening to the gentle waves.

"Much better." MT attached the wires. When she asked me to open wide, I cringed. I hated this part—the breathing tube down my throat. It was almost as bad as the fluid that would replace the air in my lungs. I tensed, though MT reminded me to relax. Who could relax when a thick gel was shoving all the air out of your lungs? I gagged, as I did in the sims. My lungs tried to reject the gel. I panicked as blackness crept in until finally my lungs adapted to this new source of oxygen.

"Sweet dreams, Commander," MT said.

"They cannot dream." Hal was such a spoilsport.

"What do you know?" MT retorted. "You're nothing but circuit boards and metal chips."

I wanted to tell them to quit bickering and pay attention to my vitals. Then their voices faded, and everything dimmed. The last thing I heard was the snick of the lock sealing me inside my tube.

En route to Serenity

Do you hear me, sweetheart? C'mon, Sara. Talk to me.

I shouldn't be able to hear him calling me. Still, I searched for his voice.

Marsh?

I'm here, babe. I hoped we'd be able to connect.

His face—his beautiful face with its hard planes and that little dimple he insisted was just a crease in his left cheek—hovered above me. I caressed the dimple and traced the arch of his right eyebrow, the one with the small scar at the tip, where his best friend hit him with a plastic light saber when they were eight.

But the psychologists say this is impossible. How can I touch you? You feel real, yet I know you can't be. You're in a cryotube at the end of the corridor.

What do the psychs know? He tapped my lips with his long, strong fingers. I kissed them, wanting to feel his caress. He smoothed my forehead. *Don't frown. You'll get wrinkles.*

His deep chuckle sounded the same as always. I fretted about my mind playing tricks on me. I was hallucinating. I couldn't really feel his face. I couldn't hear him. I was dreaming about the man I've loved for years. My new husband.

Sara, come back. Don't pull away from me.

Go away. You are an illusion.

Babe, remember that old movie The Matrix?

Why are you thinking about old movies?

I want to make a point. Remember how Morpheus took Neo into the construct room while their bodies were still in chairs on the ship? That must be where we are— on some plane of our existence. Our bodies are in the tubes, yet we're, uh, somewhere else.

I'm hallucinating. You are not real. Go away.

He straightened then held his hand out to me. Automatically, I reached for it. *No, this was a dream.* I dropped my hand.

Come on, babe. Put your hand in mine. We belong together. Not in separate tubes.

What? You think they should build double-size cryotubes so lovers can be together? Yeah, right.

I could put that suggestion in my report.

Don't you dare.

Still, I clasped his hand. Immediately, his fingers curled around my wrist, and he easily pulled me out of my tube. We were in a white space, like that room in that old science fiction movie. I didn't know what we were standing on, but it was white, too. Marsh enfolded me in his arms. With his hand cupping the back of my head, he pulled me closer still. He pressed my head against his broad chest, and I heard the steady beat of his heart. With Marsh, I was safe.

As Mission Commander, I had to be strong, in charge. Knowing he would never betray me, I could be myself. I could let my insecurities hang out.

I bet the Powers That Be didn't think about this. His chuckle rumbled in his chest under my ear.

How would they? We're the first. We'll have to tell them to prepare future teams.

I'm sure not putting this in my report. Neither are you.

Why not? We have to report everything.

Because I don't want to share this time with anyone except you.

I don't understand. And then I did as he slipped the skinny strap of my unitard off my left shoulder. *Marsh, behave.*

Why? He gave me that devilish grin.

Can't you think of anything else but sex?

Hey, I'm a guy.

He slid the other strap off then pulled my suit down to my waist. *Beautiful as always, my love.* He palmed my breast, and I shivered in anticipation. He didn't disappoint. He kissed my nipple before drawing it into his mouth.

Holding his head against me, I moaned. *Please, Marsh. Please.*

He yanked my suit down my legs. For balance as I stepped out of the thin garment, I put my hand on his bare shoulder. He held me tight against him, flesh against flesh. For a moment, I wondered when he removed his little suit, then all thoughts fled as he kissed me. Eagerly, I returned the kiss. It intensified until all I wanted was to mate with him.

I reached between us and took him into my hand.

Slow down, babe. No rush.

Still, he laid me on that white floor that wasn't a floor. With his tongue and fingers, he leisurely explored my body, as we'd done often in the past. I tried to do the same with him, but he chided me to let him do all the work. *You can have your wicked way with me when I'm done.*

When he had my body thrumming with desire, he entered me, setting off sparks of energy.

Marsh, no. We can't do this. I tried to twist away even though my body yearned for this connection. A connection we both craved yet never had.

He clasped my face between his palms. *This isn't real, Sara. Nothing can happen.*

I held him with all my might. Finally, I figured out his rhythm and matched it.

We'd never done this before, yet it felt
natural. As if we were long-time lovers. We
were, just not like this. I felt him tense.
Under my fingers, his back slicked with
sweat. He was about to come, and I was
nowhere near ready.

As if reading my mind, he worked his
hand between us and found that special
spot. *Don't worry, babe. I'm not blasting
off without you.*

Silly man. Of course he wouldn't leave
me behind. Together, we soared.

Astir

"Commander, this is your wake-up call," Hal intoned impatiently, as if that wasn't the first time he'd called.

I was in the middle of another dream with Marsh and really hated the interruption.

"Wakey, wakey. Eggs and bakey." That was MT.

Then it hit me. They were waking me. That meant the freezing mechanisms were turned off, and my body was slowly warming up. No wonder I was aware. Had the dreams of Marsh making love to me started as I returned to consciousness? Or did I have them the entire time? It felt as if they were recurring dreams. Not just a one-time deal.

MT began disengaging all the tubes and wires. "It's beginning to look a lot like Christmas," she sang as she worked. Then she switched to "Santa Claus is coming tonight."

As if her pulling the tube out of my throat wasn't bad enough, or my lungs expelling the gel, my chest hurt worse with my first real breath in three years. They told us we might be nauseous and uncomfortable after cryosleep. Might be? That was like saying childbirth was mild discomfort—not that I'd ever experienced that phenomenon. Yet.

Dizziness swept over me, and I hadn't even moved.

"We'll get you all fixed up for Santa, Commander." MT gently wiped my face. My eyes had difficulty focusing, but I thought she winked. Then she started singing "Rocking Around the Christmas Tree."

It dawned on me that she was walking, not floating, around me. Artificial gravity must have been restored. That was the plan. Since neither she nor Hal needed gravity, it had been turned off to save fuel while we were in cryo. Without the extra fuel plus no food or oxygen for six people, the lightened ship could go faster.

Still, I wished I'd been awake during the flight. Seeing the stars and planets up close would have been a tremendous thrill.

"Where are we?" The noise that came out of my dry throat sounded like a bullfrog.

"You have many questions, Commander Grenard," Hal intoned. "The date is 24 December 2175. As you know, we use Earth time in flight. When you reach—"

"Hal, you dope. She knows all that."

"I am attempting to orient her."

Three years since we left Titan Station. I'd been a popsicle for three years. No wonder I was shivering. Of course the fact that I was now naked—MT had just peeled off my unitard—might have had something to do with being cold. I was glad MT looked like a girl. I pretended Hal couldn't see me.

At least we'd be awake for Christmas. All of us. As mission commander, I was last in, first out. The others would soon join me. I couldn't wait. I couldn't imagine celebrating the holiday alone. Alone out in the black with only a computer and an android for company.

"We are one ship day from our destination," Hal continued.

Hang on. According to plan, we should be in orbit around Serenity, ready to land. Our new planet's first human inhabitants. During the final planning stage, we talked about the first holiday on our new planet. Supplies had been sent ahead. The cargo containers would be our homes until we built permanent ones. We planned every detail, from decorations to our celebratory meal in our habitats. Disappointment oozed through me that we wouldn't accomplish our goal.

"You must wonder why our arrival was delayed," Hal said.

"She doesn't need to know everything all at once," MT protested. "She needs time to—"

Yes, I wanted to know. I needed to know everything that had happened to our

ship since going into cryo. Hal understood.
MT didn't.

Since my throat hurt, I lifted my hand
to encourage Hal to continue. My hand
reacted like cooked spaghetti and fell to my
side.

"We were delayed because a near
collision with an asteroid necessitated a
course correction." Was that defiance in
Hal's voice? Then I recalled the bickering
between him and MT before I slipped into
sleep. Maybe three years asleep wasn't such
a bad idea. I couldn't imagine listening to
them all the way to Serenity.

"You idiot. Give her a chance to wake
up."

"I am not an idiot," Hal responded with
righteous indignation. "Nor am I a dope or
a dunce. I am the most sophisticated
instrument Haleogin Industries ever
constructed."

MT rolled her eyes. "He really has an
overinflated ego, you know. He thinks he
knows everything, and doesn't hesitate to
share that opinion."

"I do not," Hall huffed. "It is my
purpose to utilize my superior intellect."

MT snorted. "Superior intellect, my ass.
He is so full of himself." She tucked her
arm under my shoulder to help me into a
sitting position. "Now, upsy daisy."

Retching wracked my body. Vertigo
threatened to topple me over the edge of
my cryotube.

"Easy, Commander. Just take it easy." MT held me steady. For a little thing, she was quite strong. "You'll be right as rain in a jiffy."

I wanted to ask how she knew, but my throat hurt too much. She placed a flex tube in my mouth. "This will feel good. You don't have to sip. Close your lips around the tube and let the liquid flow naturally."

Oh my God, that did feel good. Greedily, I swallowed again and again. The sweet cool liquid coated my throat. I could see more clearly now, too. The gray walls, the narrow space through which MT maneuvered around the cryotube, the monitors with green on black readouts of my functions. Nothing had changed since I climbed into the tube. Not that I expected it to. We'd practiced so many times that I knew the location of every instrument by heart.

"That is enough for now." MT removed the drink.

I moaned in protest.

"I know. You are dehydrated, and your throat hurts. Give me a few minutes, and you can have as much to drink as you wish."

"It is my duty to inform you—"

"No, Hal." MT whirled around to face the comm unit on the wall. "Wait until she is back to normal."

"But—"

"No. You must give her time to orient herself."

"I—" I cleared my gravelly throat. "I need to know. What happened?"

"Hah!" Hal sounded triumphant. As if he'd gotten his way over MT's protests.

There I went again, giving Hal and MT human-like attributes. When machines, especially artificial intelligence, spoke like humans, it was difficult not to.

"A malfunction occurred in the cryotubes."

No. My mind cried out when my vocal cords didn't respond to my brain's command.

"Damn it, Hal. You're scaring her."

What happened? I wanted to ask yet was afraid of the answer. The six of us were pioneers to an alien planet. Dependent on each other. We were more than colleagues on a dangerous journey. We were a family.

That wasn't the only reason. Marsh.

Please, God. Let Marsh be safe. Guilt swamped me. *I'm selfish. What kind of Christmas spirit do I have to be willing to sacrifice the others so that my love could live?*

"Malfunction?" I managed to croak. I struggled to rise, tried to pull myself up by grasping the tube's rail. So weak, I fell back against the thin pad I'd lain on for three years, jarring my head.

"Commander Grenard, you must take it easy." MT patted my arm. "Hal, you dope. Why did you have to tell her like that?"

"She is in charge of the mission. I must give her all the information."

"Help me up, MT," I demanded in a whispery voice that even a bunny wouldn't obey. I had to see for myself. I had to see what happened and to whom.

"Commander, the mal—"

"No." I tried to signal to Hal to make him stop talking. Instead, my hand flopped back in my lap as before. Damn weakness. "Get me out of here. Right now." That was more like it. My voice had regained some strength, unlike the rest of me.

"But, Commander—"

"That's an order, MT."

"Yes, ma'am." She helped me swing my legs over the side. I barely felt her hands. But when my legs dangled, pins and needles jabbed at my thighs, then my calves, and finally my feet. Oh, God, that hurt.

Determined to discover if Marsh was alive, I stifled my cry of pain. If MT knew how much I hurt, she would rebuckle the restraints to keep me down. I kicked my feet and slapped my thighs, anything to return feeling to my extremities. I had to be able to stand or MT wouldn't take me to see the others. I craned my head, trying to see the tubes down the long, narrow walkway. None of the lids were raised.

Oh, dear God. Did Marsh survive? Did anyone?

"Commander—" Hal began.

"Stop. I will see for myself."

MT pulled a light green gown over my head, letting it pool at my waist. "Are you sure you want to get up? You should take it slowly. Now sit here quietly while I get an anti-grav transport." She bustled away.

"No, MT," I called after her. "I will walk. Come back and help me."

"She thinks she knows best," Hal said in a snide tone. "She is extremely irritating. You would not believe the arguments we—"

"Shut up, you hunk of junk." MT returned, lightly steering a pallet that hovered at waist height.

I raised my hand to my temple. "Enough. You two are giving me a headache. MT, I said no transport. I need to walk. I have to see—" My voice cracked. I swallowed hard to hold back my scattered emotions.

After releasing the transport, MT put my hands on her shoulders then supported me as I slipped over the edge of the cryotube. My knees had the structural stability of Jell-O. I clung to her shoulders, aware that her slenderness was deceptive. Even though I was six inches taller and forty pounds heavier, she held me up.

The metal grating of the floor cut into my bare feet. I shivered at the cold. Maybe I should use the anti-grav transport. No.

What kind of a commander gave in to discomfort when the fate of her crew remained a mystery?

Doubts assailed me. I should have allowed Hal to give his report. Being prepared had to be better than shock. If I told him now, he'd gloat and MT would—

I can manage. I can do this. In my mind, I sounded like *The Little Engine That Could.*

Clinging to the little med tech android and holding onto the edge of my tube, I baby-stepped to the end. From there I could reach the next tube. Gloria's. My friend, my confidante, the first one I'd told of my budding romance with Marsh. I stopped and closed my eyes. *Please, God, let her be all right.*

When I opened my eyes, I peered into her tube's face plate. Empty.

My heart stopped. *Oh no!* Her body had already been disintegrated. Her ashes streamed into space.

Clinging to MT, I hurried to the next tube and the next. Empty, like Gloria's. *No. Please, God, not all of them.*

Marsh's was the last. *I can't look. I have to.* I held onto the edge, then took a deep breath. I opened my eyes.

Empty.

My knees gave out. Despite MT's efforts, I sank to the floor. Tears streamed down my face. Grief battered my heart, squeezing, burning, until my chest felt as empty as the cryotubes.

"Commander." MT struggled to help me up.

"Leave me alone." I wrapped my arms around myself and curled up. I wanted to die right there. Our mission had failed. I was all alone. Alone in the black.

Why am I the only one left? It should have been Marsh. He was stronger. He could survive anywhere. Or Gloria. She had the biggest heart. Ana's knowledge exceeded all of ours. She should have been the one to live. Or Bill who could fix anything. Or Tom. Of all of us, he could survive in solitude.

Why me? My heart shredded, and I cried inside.

"Why are you sitting on the floor?"

I was hallucinating. That couldn't be Marsh's voice. He was gone. Like the others.

"C'mon, babe."

A dream. Like before. Strong hands lifted me up. I knew those hands, had felt them under my arms before. Felt them all over my body. Just like in my dreams. That was what this was. Another dream.

Now those hands cradled me against a hard chest. A chest beneath which beat a heart so loudly it hurt my ears. A wonderful hurt.

"It's about time you got up." His chuckle rumbled beneath my ear.

I raised my head to look into his laughing brown eyes and reached to touch his face. "You're alive."

"I'd say that was obvious." Again, he chuckled.

"B-But Hal said there was a malfunction in the tubes. I thought . . ."

"Yeah. We woke up a little early. All at once. Except you. You should have seen MT scrambling from one tube to the next."

"Wait." I held his face between my palms. "Are you saying everyone is alive?"

"And waiting for Sleeping Beauty to get her rear in gear." He urged me down the passageway to the combo gathering/dining space.

I didn't believe him. I wanted to. Hesitating in the portal, I clung to Marsh.

"Happy holidays," they shouted as he led me into the room. Laughing and cheering, the four surrounded us. Gloria and Tom, Ana and Bill. Alive. They were all alive.

After much hugging, Marsh said, "Give her some space."

"Hal." I glared at the comm speaker on the wall. "Why did you let me think they all died?"

"As I recall," the disembodied voice said with a haughty tone, "you ordered me to stop speaking."

"Yeppers," MT said from the portal. "You ordered me not to talk, too."

They were right. It was my own fault for jumping to conclusions. "My apologies."

I clung to Marsh, reluctant to let him go, even when he seated me in a chair. I stroked his face and let my hand drift down his chest. My love was still alive.

Gloria brought over a container of the same liquid MT gave me to drink. "This will help." Marsh took it from her and held it while I sipped.

She returned to Tom's side on one of the benches against the wall. Ana and Bill cuddled on the other. When I looked away from their obvious infatuation with each other, I saw the decorations. Garlands were strung around the doorframe and hung from the ceiling in loops. A small artificial tree sat on the table between the loveseats. I wondered who sneaked the tree into their gear. Sparkling lights blinked next to tiny ornaments on the tree. On another table, a menorah with electric lights and the unlit 7-candled candelabra for Kwanzaa reminded us that more holidays than Christmas were being celebrated.

Between sips of the soothing beverage, I asked, "How long have you been awake?"

Marsh answered, "Twelve hours."

"What? And no one thought I would want to be awakened, too?"

"It was my decision." Of course it would be. He was second in command. "I thought it best to let the procedure cycle normally."

"I could have slept through Christmas," I groused.

"Nah. I know how much Christmas means to you. Besides, how could I give you your present if you were still asleep?"

I brightened at that. I loved presents. More giving than getting, though. I loved watching others open my gifts and seeing their delight when I'd chosen the right thing.

"What present?" I asked as eagerly as a four-year-old.

He helped me up, then led me across the room. "Close your eyes."

"Unfair," I protested but obeyed.

With me clutching his side, we walked three more steps. He held me in front of him, his arms around my waist. He pressed his cheek against mine. "Merry Christmas, love."

I opened my eyes. We stood in front of the viewport. There, across the black. A magnificent blue sphere, with browns and greens, and scatterings of white clouds.

Serenity.

"It's beautiful."

Marsh pressed his lips against my neck. "Welcome home, love."

A New Beginning

The next morning, we climbed into our shuttle. As Tom piloted our craft through Serenity's atmosphere, the heatshield glowed hot. I glanced over at him. His knuckles were bone-white. Tom held our lives in those hands gripping the control.

Though we made it safely through the atmo, the terror continued as we plummeted toward the surface. Calmly, as the green planet rushed toward us, Bill read out the gauges, counting down the kilometers. Finally, Tom engaged the retro rockets to slow our descent. Still, we were going too fast. My turn to grip the arms of my chair until my knuckles shone white.

"Are you going to rip off that arm?" Marsh asked.

I noticed his eyes weren't twinkling despite his joking comment. We were all tense. Gloria's face was a sculpture in fright. Ana's eyes were tightly shut.

"We're coming in too hot," Marsh said with a calmness I didn't feel.

"I got it," Tom responded. "No worries."

Then the craft slowed, and he gently set us down on the surface right on target at

LZ-1. As the engine wound down, he turned to me with a serious expression. *What's wrong?* We were at the right spot. Four cargo containers sat nearby, one for each couple plus a common use container where we would work, eat, and hang out.

"Thank you for flying Serenity Air," Tom announced. "Please make sure your seats and tray tables are in their upright position before departing."

Gloria unbuckled the restraints then slapped his shoulder. "You are not funny." From behind, she wrapped her arms around his neck and plastered a big kiss on his cheek. "Thank you for not letting us die."

"Merry Christmas and happy holidays, Mission Control," I spoke into the main comm. "Adventure One has landed."

Silence greeted my message. It would take hours for the message to be relayed via satellites to Mission Control on Titan, even longer for it to reach Mars. Those on Earth would have to wait much longer for the news.

"Congratulations, Commander." Hal's voice came through the shuttle comm speaker. He and MT would stay aboard our ship on its return to Titan. "You sound very pleased."

"No shit, Sherlock," Bill said as he released his harness. He knuckled Tom's head. "You done good, Tommy-Boy."

Out of the corner of my eye, I could see Gloria wiping away tears. Relief gushed through me. We made it. Hard to believe. I felt a burning behind my own eyes.

I cleared my throat. "Marsh, what's the status of the atmosphere?"

Ever since we touched down, he'd been watching his instruments. He looked at me and grinned. "Conducive to humans."

"Let's not take any chances," I warned. "We wear our enviro suits and helmets."

"Yeah," Bill said. "Don't want the first vids from Serenity to be of us kicking the bucket the minute we step out of the module."

"Thanks, Bill, for that visual," I drawled.

"Keep your face shields up so the lucky people on Earth can see our smiling faces," Marsh said.

"Men," Ana said in disgust.

I agreed but refrained from saying so.

We each expressed our relief in different ways. Women cried, men joked.

When we were all suited up and helmets secured, I looked at the crew. "Ready, team?"

Tom popped the hatch and lowered the ramp. "After you, Commander."

As mission commander, it was my privilege to go first. I walked down the ramp and took my first step onto the alien planet.

I turned to the others who followed me . . . and the vids recording our movements. "Welcome to Serenity, our new home."

So prosaic. Although I'd wracked my brain for months during training, I knew I couldn't top Neil Armstrong's "One small step for man . . ."

We stood on a broad grassy plain. Trees were a good distance away with a large lake nearby. The landing zone was chosen for its lack of obstacles to interfere with the cargo landings, our landing, too. I was overwhelmed with emotion. This planet teemed with life—plants and, if the scurrying sounds were correct—animals. My mind whirled at the prospect of making our home here.

My instruments indicated the air was breathable. The perfect mix of nitrogen, oxygen, and carbon dioxide—just as the probe reported, and Marsh's instruments verified. Gravity—as we discovered while walking off the shuttle—was close to that of Earth. And the temperature was sixty-five degrees Fahrenheit. Could it be more perfect?

As team leader, I removed my helmet first. A cool breeze dried the nervous sweat on my face. When I took my first breath, I was reminded of the hills above my home. Sweet, clean air. The first I'd felt for over two years.

"Well?" Bill asked. "Are you going to pass out or what?"

Knowing we were being filmed for transmission back to Earth, I couldn't pretend to collapse. "Remove your helmets, and see for yourself."

Eagerly, they all did so. The smiles on their faces told the same story. Gratitude. Amazement. Wonder.

We'd done it. Serenity was the perfect planet for Earth's inhabitants.

Before leaving Titan, I'd prepared two statements. I was so glad I wouldn't have to use the second—the one about failure.

My team was wandering around checking out our new home. I hated to intrude, but the people back home were waiting. I set up the recording device. To this point, vids from our ship had been streaming back to Earth via the stations on Titan and Mars. Our fellow Terrans needed to hear from us directly.

"It's time, folks." I gathered the team around me so we faced the shuttle camera. "To the people of Earth. We have found our new home. In the coming days, we will report what we find here on Serenity. We give thanks to those who made our journey possible. We appreciate all your thoughts and prayers for our safety. Please continue for the other teams. Good-bye from Landing Zone One on Serenity."

As soon as I ended the transmission, I called Hal on my wrist comm. "Did you get that?"

"Of course, Commander. I am pleased to report that your transmission is winging its way to Earth."

Winging? I think some of MT's insouciance had rubbed off on him. "Good. Do you have anything else to report?"

"Yes. According to the last transmission from Titan, the mega-transports will be ready for launch a year ahead of schedule. The Exodus will begin in approximately eight months."

"What about the other teams?" I asked. "Have they reached their destinations?"

"Yes, Commander. Planet 6719 proved uninhabitable."

I could almost feel Yuri's disappointment. I knew how I would feel if Serenity hadn't lived up to our expectations.

"The Euro-African team is headed for Planet 2247 to join the Asians. That planet is habitable, with higher gravity than Earth."

While it was good that Planet 2247, Peace, was habitable, with the higher than normal gravity, work would be more strenuous. It would also take a while to become accustomed to everything weighing more.

"Other than that," Hal continued, "nothing of significance. I have sent all reports to my counterpart on board your shuttle."

"You never told them about The Weasel." MT, onboard, giggled. I was going to miss her.

"They aren't interested in gossip." Hal again spoke with a haughty attitude.

Tom grabbed my wrist to speak into my comm. "What about The Weasel?"

"He was dismissed from the program the day after your departure," MT gloated. "Commander Pushenko reported that The Weasel tried to poison one of his teammates. The techs found footage of him putting a substance into her drink. Just like he did with Pilot Warfield. When they examined the vid footage closer, they saw him sneaking something into Pilot Warfield's drink. The Weasel was caught red-handed."

"Red-handed?" Hal scoffed. "That expression makes no sense. It does not seem appropriate to—"

"Oh, stick a cork in it, Hal," MT interrupted.

"As you will have nothing to do on the journey back to Titan, Medical Technician 447," Hal intoned, "you may shut down, and I will enjoy peace and quiet."

"And you should spend your time brushing up on human slang," MT countered.

"That is a useless endeavor as informal speech changes rapidly and—"

"Enough," I cut Hal off. In the short period of time I'd been awake, their arguments drove me crazy.

"So they caught him." Tom's lips curled in satisfaction. "Good."

Despite our intention to be as serene as the name of our planet, I agreed with Tom. Erik didn't deserve to be part of our program. He represented the worst of humankind. His desperate measures had been justly rewarded.

"What about Sharlene?" Gloria asked.

Bill and Ana looked at her in question.

MT squealed. "She had a baby girl. Her name is Serenity. Sharlene and Serenity are with her parents in the salt caves under Detroit. She told Erik he had no place in their lives."

Gloria sniffed. "I suppose he's safe and sound in a cave."

"Actually," MT said with glee. "His uncle—UESA Chief Engineering Director— was so angry with what he'd done, Erik has to wait with the general population."

"After the way he treated her, he got what he deserved," I said.

Ana and Bill looked at each other. "Okay, guys," Bill said. "What did we miss?"

"Later," I mouthed.

"Commander Grenard," Hal intoned. "We wish you and your team a long and prosperous life in your new home."

"Thank you, Hal. We wish you a safe journey back to Titan." I was surprised at my sadness that he and MT were leaving. "MT, thank you for taking care of us. We will talk to you both on your next run. Safe travels."

"Bye, team," MT said. "Don't do anything I wouldn't do."

The transmission ended in the middle of her giggle. Our ship would return to Titan and after a brief refit would return with another team. In six years.

We all looked to the azure blue sky, as if we could see our ship leaving. There went our last transport home. Not that we could return. The ship didn't have enough fuel for extra passengers. The next transport would not arrive for six years. By then, we would have either survived and flourished or . . .

"We should rename this place," Gloria interrupted my dark thoughts. "LZ-1 is so—so boring."

The others nodded.

"What about Christmas?" Ana said.

"We aren't all Christian." Bill nodded to Tom.

"Holiday?" Marsh asked.

"What do you all think of naming it Paradise?" Tom suggested.

"Perfect," Gloria said. "Just as perfect as this place seems to be."

"Watch out for snakes, though." Bill grinned.

The rest of us groaned.

"How far away do you think those mountains are?" Gloria asked.

Marsh answered, "Two-three hundred klicks. Difficult to tell. The clean atmosphere is deceptive. Could be farther."

Tom clapped him on the shoulder. "We have the rest of our lives to find out."

Back on Titan, we'd discussed what to do immediately after landing. Our discussions resumed last night. The consensus hadn't changed.

"Choose your new home," I said. "Leave one of the habitats in the middle for the common area."

While I waited for the others to choose, Marsh returned to the shuttle for pallet jacks so we could move out the crates inside the containers. The guys cleared an aisle in each container. Meanwhile, Ana, Gloria, and I opened a few of the well-marked crates with essential equipment—food, medicines, blankets, collapsible furniture.

Though the jacks did most of the work, we tired after a few hours. I called a break. "What do you think about meeting up in, say, an hour?"

"Make it two, Commander." Bill grinned. "It'll take us a while to, uh, settle in."

Ana rolled her eyes, but she grabbed a blanket and followed him to their container. Gloria glanced at me. With a twinkle in her eyes, she nodded to me. "I think Ana has a good idea."

We both grabbed blankets.

Marsh and I headed for the farthest container on the left. Once inside, I slid the door to our container closed. As the men had worked in each container, they'd turned on the lights and artificial atmosphere. Most of the mustiness had disappeared.

With my back to the door, I unfastened the top of my enviro suit. "Would you like your Christmas present now or wait until tonight?"

"Now." He followed my example with his suit. "I wondered why you didn't give me something last night." His silly grin set my heart aflutter, as it always did.

Onboard last night, we had a small celebration at midnight, singing Christmas carols and Hanukah songs plus toasting the success of our mission. I'd handed out small tokens as gifts to the others, but to Marsh I'd whispered, "Tomorrow."

"It's tomorrow. Think I could have my present now?" He reminded me of a kid who got his parents up at six on Christmas morning.

I shoved down my enviro suit, and soon we stood before each other in our working jumpsuits. I put my arms around his neck and gave him a long kiss. "I'm your present, Marsh."

Then I stepped back and reached for the fastener near my throat. Slowly, I pulled the fastener apart, one centimeter at a time. All the while I gazed into his eyes.

When his eyes darkened, a shiver of delight rippled through me, and I thought of my dreams during cryo.

Before I could tell him about my dreams, he brushed my hands aside. "I want to open my own present." He yanked apart the fastener. When he got to my waist, his eyes widened. "You aren't wearing any underwear."

I'd never gone commando in my life. Today seemed like a good time to start. I gave him a slow grin. "Why waste time?"

Within seconds, he shoved off my jumpsuit and dispensed with his own. We stood plastered to each other, skin to skin. I held his face. "Think we could get started on our mission?"

"Mission?" The disbelief in his voice made me smile. "You want to talk about our mission? Now?"

Keeping my expression bland, I said, "Yes. The mission to populate the planet."

"Oh, *that* mission. My pleasure, Commander. My pleasure." His mouth came down on mine.

We only broke apart to spread the blanket on the floor. I quivered with anticipation. Finally, we could truly make love. Wow. Did he ever know how to pleasure me. When he loomed over me, he stared into my eyes. "Are you ready for this?"

I grinned. "As ready as I'll ever be. Don't make me wait."

He didn't.

My dreams in cryo couldn't compare. His urgency and patience—a potent combination—drove me mad. I dug my fingers into his back. "Hurry."

"Good things come—" He sounded out of breath. "—to those who wait."

"Marsh, dammit. I've waited for almost six years."

"Wait no longer, my darling."

Afterward, we lay in each other's arms, squeezed between crates containing clothing and gardening equipment.

"I think something is poking me," I said. When Marsh gave me an idiotic grin, I said, "Not *that*. In my butt. I think it's a splinter."

He rolled me toward him to examine my backside. "No splinter." He felt around on the floor. "A joint in the flooring. Sorry, sweetheart. I should have found a bed."

"I don't know about you, but I couldn't have waited until you found a bed."

"You're right. As always. I couldn't have waited any longer, either." Leaning over me, he pressed his lips against the tender spot. "Mmm. I don't think I've kissed you there before."

I pushed him up. "You were too busy getting down to business."

"Is that a complaint? I say we find a bed in this mess. And get back to business."

"Forget the bed for now." I cuddled against him. After a pause, I traced squiggly lines on his chest. "While we were in cryo, did you dream?"

"There are no dreams in cryo," he parroted the scientists.

"I know that's what they said. They lied. I dreamed."

He shook his head.

"I did, Marsh. I dreamed of you. I dreamed you came to me, and we made love. For real."

He arched his split eyebrow. "Wet dreams in space?"

My cheeks burned.

"Did you?" he needled. When I didn't respond, he waited for several moments. "I dreamed, too."

"You did? What did you dream about?"

"Fishing."

"What!" I batted his shoulder. "I dreamed of you, and you dreamed of fish?"

A slow grin began to crease his face. "I lied. I dreamed of Christmas and presents . . . and you."

Day 1 . . . of the rest of our lives

Marsh prodded me. "We should explore."

Even though I knew he was right, I want to stay in his arms.

With a longing look at his magnificent body, I pulled on my jumpsuit. Together, we walked out in time to see a setting sun. Our teammates were already exploring. Ana had walked several meters away from the camp, checking out a clump of what looked like wildflowers. We'd brought seeds from home. Until they were planted and harvested, we'd have to depend on dried rations. We all hoped that Ana would find edible flora and fauna to supplement our rations.

Bill and Tom chatted in front of the cargo unit next to ours—the module no one took. Bill gestured expansively while Tom listened. Gloria sat at a small table with a bucket next to her. She was examining water under her microscope.

"Hey, sleepyheads," Bill called out to us. "Come and see what's in this cargo unit."

He pointed to the module next to ours, the one we hadn't started to empty. As part of our training, we were given a list of the contents. I wasn't surprised to see a surface vehicle. We would use the shuttle for long trips, exploring this continent and the two others. The surface vehicle would do for short hops, especially useful for hauling. Someone back on Titan had decorated the front of the it. 'California or Bust.' California was X-ed out and under it was written 'Serenity.'

Bill pointed. "That's not all. Look at the side."

I craned my head. 'Live long and prosper' with the Vulcan peace sign was painted on the door. A good sentiment.

Turning to the two guys, I said, "Okay. What were you talking about?"

"Our first building." With a stick, Bill sketched in the dirt, his engineering background evident in his drawing. "A town hall."

"That's super," I said. "I'm pleased you're coming up with plans."

"What did you think I was doing on Titan? I have plans for all the buildings we'll need."

"Good, because I bet the other two teams we'd have our settlement up first." I grinned.

"You what?" Bill gave me the stink eye.

I laughed. "You heard me. I have confidence in my team."

"I guess we'd better get going," Bill groused.

Tom clapped him on the back. "You know what they say. No rest for the weary."

Gloria came up. "I've tested the water from the lake. I want to do more testing, but it looks like there are no parasites or bacteria. The water may be drinkable."

Another positive for our landing site. Two large containers of water and a filtration unit had been sent ahead with the cargo. To find potable water close by was a bonus.

During our first meal in our new home—reconstituted turkey and dressing and tofurkey for Ana, the vegetarian—we talked about our expectations and reality. Our new home was better than anticipated.

Ana summed up what I was thinking. "Is this place too good to be true?"

"Don't knock it, baby." Bill leaned over and gave her a smacking kiss.

"Ana's right. We can't let ourselves be lulled into complacency." Marsh warned. "Expect the unexpected."

Gloria groaned. "Can't we just enjoy our meal without worrying about the future?"

Marsh's mouth twisted in chagrin. "You're right. Just saying, we need to be prepared for surprises."

I stopped eating. "He is right. We've seen the satellite pictures and know what to expect regarding weather conditions."

Currently, this continent in Serenity's southern hemisphere was experiencing spring. The worst season, according to the reports, was fall. Winter, however, did not appear to have the extreme temperature changes that the middle latitudes on Earth experienced. I hoped this temperate weather would continue.

"Okay, Number Two, we'll be alert." Bill gave Marsh a mock salute.

"Was that a *Star Trek* reference?" Marsh grinned widely.

"Just quoting Captain Picard."

Those two watched endless vids of the ancient television and movie series. I loved movies but nothing like they did. If they saw a chance to repeat a quote, they didn't hesitate.

"I feel bad for Yuri's team," Ana said. "We're lucky Serenity doesn't have noxious air or vicious animals."

Marsh nodded. "We *are* the lucky ones. We escaped the old Earth. And here we are on New Earth, Serenity. Humankind has a chance. I'm just thankful we made it."

Tom rose from our make-shift table— three crates pushed together. "As you already know, I've never been a religious man." He'd made that clear on many occasions. "This voyage has changed me. Since we came out of cryo, I keep thanking God for letting us survive. Now I thank Him . . . or Her—" He glanced at Gloria who had strong beliefs about gender neutrality with regard to the Supreme Being. "—for providing humankind with a new beginning. May we not screw it up the way we did Earth."

After a moment of stunned silence, Bill held up his glass of reconstituted grape juice. "To our new home. Serenity. May God bless us all."

Note from Diane

Thank you for reading **Mission to New Earth.** I hope you enjoyed it. Authors love reviews. Please let others know what you thought of this book by leaving a review at Goodreads and/or your favorite online retailer.

Turn the page for a quick look at

The Protector
An Outer Rim Novel

by Diane Burton

CHAPTER 1

After cutting the heel off a loaf of jambor, Rissa Dix sat on a stool at her work island, closed her eyes, and inhaled the scent of freshly-baked bread. Along with her third cup of sheelonga tea, she ate the warm bread with its distinctive nutty taste.

Her Mid-Day indulgence. The only time she rested. From early morning until she closed at Mid-Night, she rarely sat. Too much to do, so little time.

The tavern had done well last night. The Winslott miners had wound down, as they usually did midway into their furlough. For the first tenday, they blew off steam, drank, and feasted. The next few days would be the same until they realized it was nearly time to return to the lambidium mines. Then they would drink more than they should and try to get in as many visits as possible to Fortuna's Pleasure Palace across the street.

As Rissa savored her treat, her comm beeped from where she'd left it on the counter near the cooler. Normally she wore the device on her wrist just not while making jambor. No sense getting it clogged up with flour. She spun on the stool and stretched to reach the comm.

When she saw Ropergor's gray face in the mini-monitor, she answered, "Hey, how's my favorite traffic controller?"

"Mistress Rissa." The Volpian's long, gray chin wobbled. *"Do you have any food or ale you can spare? A transport landed last night for repairs and they want to stock up before they leave. The mechs finished repairs on the hydraulic leak, and the pilot is ready to go. I tried Chef Nalgin, but he's in the middle of the café's Mid-Day rush."*

"How much do they want?" She and the owner of the café often supplied ships but usually with more notice.

Ropergor told her quantities. *"It must have a larger crew than I've seen."*

"No problem." As she talked, she headed toward the stairs beyond the bar. "We can be there in twenty mins."

After disconnecting, she rapped on the door to Kiran's quarters. "I need some help," she called to her bartender.

A groggy Kiran opened the door. While scrubbing his bald head, he ducked under the frame then straightened to his full height. Zeboris usually went around two meters tall. Kiran was more than two and a half. Broad shouldered, with skin as black as a manval, and teeth just as white and sharp, he could be terrifying when angered. That made him a great bouncer. Not that *she* couldn't handle a drunken miner or two.

"Whassup, Boss?" Kiran voice was so deep it seemed to come from his toes.

Thank the Matriarch he'd thrown on one of his short wrap-around, native skirts—tan with dark blue Zebori symbols.

"Some numbnut pilot wants provisions. Now."

"He should have thought ahead." Kiran smothered a yawn.

Rissa couldn't believe it when he ducked back into his quarters. "Hey. I need help now."

He turned around, his hand on the closure to his skirt, his black eyes twinkling. "Figured I'd better dress appropriately."

"Uh, yeah. Hurry up, okay?"

When she bent down to reach into the storage area under the bar, her long braid fell over her shoulder. *Darn thing.* One day she'd cut it off. She pulled out an anti-grav pallet then guided it to the kitchen. Within mins, Kiran showed up wearing traditional Rimmer garb—multi-pocketed shirt and trousers in dun-colored coarse-spun. Same as hers.

She and Kiran loaded four loaves of fresh jambor, two dozen turken eggs, a large tub of frozen hican stew, and a case of Astron Ale onto the pallet. She left a note and the alley door unlocked for Sophira who could handle the few miners that might wander in. Rissa doubted many would show up. Most were sleeping off last night's indulgences.

She and Kiran made it to the spaceport with two mins to spare.

As soon as she entered the enclosed hangar, the smells assaulted her nose the way they always did. Lubricating fluid and ferranite dust were bad enough, but the cloyingly sweet odor of barzilium overpowered all. Servo-bots were transferring the bars of fuel from a stack against the left wall onto a waiting freighter.

Traffic Controller Ropergor minced up to her. "Thank the Divine One you've come. The pilot is quite anxious to get underway."

He guided her to an old freighter, its hull a shade lighter than the rust around the hatch. A grizzled Chellian in a wrinkled spacer uniform stood at the entrance to the airlock. The faded spots across his forehead and down the sides of his face indicated he was almost as old as his ship. He shifted from one foot to the other.

As she and Kiran approached with the supplies, the spacer strode down the ramp. "It's about time you got here. We're ready to get off this rock."

Rissa put her hands on her hips. "Most pilots give advanced notice for supplies."

"Yeah, yeah. Just bring the stuff aboard."

When he started to go back into his ship, she called out, "After you pay for it."

He returned quickly enough. After she told him the amount, she held out her credit device. She'd only been burned once by a crew who refused to pay after she'd already unloaded their supplies. She'd learned her lesson and always got payment first.

"That much? That's robbery."

"I can take it back to the tavern." She motioned to Kiran to back away.

"All right, all right." The pilot keyed in his info and the amount before slamming the small box into her hand. "I still say it's robbery."

The pilot's attitude grated on her nerves. He'd already interrupted her quiet time. Now he was complaining.

"Extra charge for rush deliveries."

While backing out of their way, he grumbled curses. Rissa had heard worse. She followed Kiran as he guided the AG pallet into the ship. Typical freighter set up. The airlock opened to a corridor. Bridge on the right, galley down and on the left. Kiran steered the pallet toward the galley.

"That's far enough." The pilot's abrupt command stopped them from going farther. "Take the boxes off the pallet and leave them on the deck."

"In the middle of the corridor?" Rissa asked.

"My crew will take everything into the galley."

All the time she and the pilot had talked—argued—two Chellian crewmen stood at the entrance to the bridge and stared at her, lasciviousness in their eyes. For the first time in ages a man made her feel unclean. The space crews and miners who frequented her tavern treated her with respect.

The faster she got off this ship the better. She and Kiran quickly unloaded the pallet. As if using mental telepathy, neither bothered to leave a walkway between the boxes and the walls. She was only too happy to let the crew do the lifting and carrying. Considering how much food they'd ordered, the rest of the crew must be working elsewhere on the ship.

"You there, Zebbie." The pilot pointed to Kiran. "Hurry up."

"You will speak to him with respect," Rissa snapped. "Or forget getting any supplies the next time you come here."

The pilot sneered. "I won't stop here again. You people are all crooks. Do you know how much they charged me for patching up a tiny leak? And you." He pointed at her. "You've got a lot of nerve gouging me for a little food."

Before she could lambaste the pilot, Kiran took her arm, steering the pallet with his other hand. "Time to go, Boss. We're done here."

They were done, all right. She'd warn Chef Nalgin and Merchant Graeson about this pilot. They didn't need his business.

After they left the ship, Rissa told Kiran to take the pallet back to the tavern while she had a word with Traffic Controller Ropergor. First, though, she needed the sanitary facility to wash off the stench from the pilot and his leering crew.

When Rissa entered the unisex sanfac, the odors made her gag. The mechanics had left their calling cards—grease and dirt smudges—in the sinks, on the counters and on the doors to the stalls. She doubted a place this dirty would wash away anything. It looked like the room hadn't been cleaned in years. Next time, she'd use the san-fac out in the passenger waiting area.

She washed her hands then realized there was no towel. Her trousers would have to do. As she turned to leave, she heard a rustle in the stall nearest the wall. When she checked under the door, she couldn't see feet. Hair on the back of her neck rose in alarm. Immediately, she looked up in case some *thing* was about to pounce on her.

She stepped back. "Pacer, you stupid space jock. You'd better not be looking over the partition."

Silence. Probably wasn't Pacer. He would've strolled out with a smart answer.

"Whoever you are, come out. Right now."

Another rustle then the sound of feet lightly hitting the floor. The lock slid open then slowly the door moved.

"Please," a soft voice whispered. "Don't hurt us."

That sounded like a young girl.

"Come out where I can see you." Rissa, too, whispered.

A tall, dark-haired teen stepped out, followed by a smaller girl with light brown hair. They both looked terrified. Their hair was matted and dirt smudged their faces. Their clothes were filthy. The smells emanating from them contributed to the general san-fac odors. Rissa did her best not to react.

Holding the other girl behind her, the tall one stepped forward, jutting out her chin. "We are not going back."

"O-kay. Back where?"

"You can't make us. We'll escape again."

Rissa had to admire her bravado. "You escaped? From where?"

"Did they send you in here to get us?"

Since the taller one seemed to be the spokesperson, Rissa kept her eyes on her. Something about her was compelling. Rissa could be looking at herself at the same age. Then it hit her hard, like a blow to the stomach. That was what Miri would have looked like at that age. Same strong Traishan features—olive skin, dark hair and eyes. Same strong will.

Rissa took a deep breath to steady herself before locking the outer door. "Nobody sent me. You asked for help. What can I do?"

"Get us out of here before they discover we're gone." Despite the strength in the tall girl's voice, she worked hard to keep her chin from wobbling.

"Who?" Rissa was afraid she knew.

"Those men. The Chellians. We can't go back. We won't."

By the Matriarch, traffickers.

Her lungs seized, her heart hurt so badly Rissa clutched her chest. *Be strong*, she told herself. *Pull yourself together.* No traffickers had ever come to Astron Colony before. Or even to Galeriana. She had to help the girls get away.

Look for The Protector and other Outer Rim Novels at your favorite retailer.

About the Author

Diane Burton combines her love of mystery, adventure, science fiction and romance into writing romantic fiction. Besides the science fiction romance *Switched* and *Outer Rim* series, she writes romantic suspense and cozy mysteries (The Alex O'Hara Novels). She is also a contributor to to two anthologies, *How I Met My Husband* and *Portals, Volume 2*. Diane and her husband live in Michigan. They have two children and five grandchildren.

For more info and excerpts from her books, visit Diane's website: http://www.dianeburton.com

Connect with Diane Burton online

Blog: dianeburton.blogspot.com/
Facebook: Diane Burton Author
Twitter: @dmburton72
Pinterest: dmburton72
Goodreads: Diane Burton Author

If you would like to know when a new book is released, sign up for Diane's newsletter. http://eepurl.com/bdHtYf

www.ingramcontent.com/pod-product-compliance
Lightning Source LLC
Chambersburg PA
CBHW060622130626
46555CB00002B/611